Nate Shepard was everything Miranda had ever thought she wanted in a man

He made plans sporadically and changed them on a whim. He lived on the edge and loved it. He answered to no one but himself, took pleasure where he found it and made no apology for it. Life was big and he was living it.

It took less than twenty-four hours for his joie de vivre to drive Miranda crazy.

She didn't know how anyone could live at such a pace. She didn't understand, or much appreciate, his style of spontaneity. She didn't care if his glamorous lifestyle wasn't—as he put it—all it was cracked up to be. She only knew she couldn't live that way. She needed routine, schedules, plans. She needed stability and steadiness. She needed...Nate.

She longed for him with a frightening intensity, missed him as if he'd been out of her life for months instead of hours. And although she told herself she had what she wanted, in the early-morning dusk of a new day she acknowledged that she might have made a terrible mistake.

THE MATCHMAKER'S SISTER
Karen Toller Whittenburg

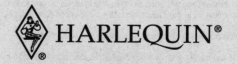

TORONTO • NEW YORK • LONDON
AMSTERDAM • PARIS • SYDNEY • HAMBURG
STOCKHOLM • ATHENS • TOKYO • MILAN • MADRID
PRAGUE • WARSAW • BUDAPEST • AUCKLAND

ISBN 0-373-75014-5

THE MATCHMAKER'S SISTER

Copyright © 2004 by Karen Whittenburg Crane.

This edition published by arrangement with Harlequin Books S.A.

Visit us at www.eHarlequin.com

Printed in U.S.A.

ABOUT THE AUTHOR

Karen Toller Whittenburg credits her love of reading with
inspiring her writing career. She enjoys fiction in every form,
but romance continues to hold a special place for her. As a
teenager she spent long, lovely hours falling in love with
Emilie Loring's heroines, falling in love with every hero and
participating in every adventure. It's no wonder she always
dreamed of being a romance writer. Karen lives in
Oklahoma and divides her time between writing and running a household, both full-time and fulfilling careers.

Books by Karen Toller Whittenburg

HARLEQUIN AMERICAN ROMANCE

Don't miss any of our special offers. Write to us at the
following address for information on our newest releases.

Harlequin Reader Service
U.S.: 3010 Walden Ave., P.O. Box 1325, Buffalo, NY 14269
Canadian: P.O. Box 609, Fort Erie, Ont. L2A 5X3

Monday, August 4

12:15   Lunch with Ainsley @ Torrid Tomato.
Re: WEDDING

Items To Discuss/**Decisions MUST be made TODAY.

1. Date/time**
   a. October 31st too soon/not enough time to plan!
      1) need at least 18 months
      2) Halloween! (No, no, no, no, no!)
   b. Time of Ceremony
      1) Evening 8:30 (8?)

2. Place—Newport Methodist. No discussion allowed.

3. No. of Attendants** (Must be four or six. Not three or five.)
   a. Candlelighters (More than two is tacky.)
   b. Children?
      1) Calvin Braddock—ring bearer?
         a) Adam and Katie's little girl, Janey, too young for flower girl.
         b) Does Ivan have a suitable family relation?
      2) Children misbehave/create disruptions

4. Florist**
   a. My area of expertise
      1) My friend Cleo (First choice)
      2) Victoria (If Cleo unavailable)

5. Photographer/Videographer**
   a. Andrew's area of expertise
      1) Contract/deposit?
      2) Consultation meeting?
      3) Portrait sitting—No discussion!

6. Reception**
   a. Danfair—talk to Matt about date; put on his calendar!
      1) If country club preferred, contact Jacques immediately!
      2) Caterer**
         a) Menu
         b) Wine list
   b. Entertainment**
      1) Music selection

7. Miscellaneous
   a. Invitations**
      1) Calligrapher
   b. Guest List
      1) Deadline—1 week!!

8. TOO MANY DETAILS—TOO LITTLE TIME!!
   a. Must persuade A & I to change date.

9. Buy Aspirin.
   a. Ask Dr. Ivan how many constitute lethal dose.
   b. Don't take that many.

Chapter One

Miranda Danville knew how to plan a wedding.

She'd never actually done so, but, really, how hard could it be? Especially for someone with her organizational skills. Planning anything successfully—be it a full-scale wedding or the layout of a breathtaking garden—was simply a matter of making a list. Or several lists, depending on the size and time constraints of the project. Then items on the list—or lists—prioritized by importance, organized by category and subclassified according to when and/or where action was required. There had to be some flexibility, of course, but successful planning essentially consisted of making and following a list.

A concept that was obviously unfamiliar to the wedding planner who'd put together today's fiasco. Even taking into account the last-minute nature of the occasion—Miranda's cousin, Scott, and his bride, Molly, had nearly married once before, but at the last minute and for reasons still unclear to Miranda, the bride had developed cold feet, decided she wasn't good enough for Scott and instead of walking down the aisle, she'd hit the front door running. Miranda wasn't exactly clear, either, on how the two had reconnected, although she attributed some of the blame or the credit—depending on which family member she was talking with—to her sister, Ainsley, who was, as improbable as it still seemed to Miranda, an apprentice matchmaker.

But however the reunion had come about, once Scott and Molly found each other again, they weren't taking any chances and wanted to have the wedding they'd missed out on two months before immediately. If not sooner. Which Miranda conceded was a tall order for anyone, although in her humble opinion, that neither explained nor acquitted the person or persons who had arranged this event. The wedding that had taken place earlier in the evening had contained some major faux pas. Mistakes that almost certainly could have been prevented, even at short notice, if the wedding planner had taken the time to compile a comprehensive list.

The worst, however, turned out to be the reception, held at Oceanview, the Cliffside mansion Miranda's uncle Edward called his cabin by the sea, where the food was going faster than the buffet line. Any wedding planner worth her consulting fee might be forgiven for the unfortunate incident with the candles—the fire, after all, had been minor—and perhaps there had been no way to avoid the mix-up with the flowers or to prevent the fracas between the organist, the flautist, the soloist and the cellist.

But there was no excuse for the shortage of food.

Well, no one would have the opportunity to mess up Ainsley's wedding. It was going to be perfect. Absolutely perfect. The wedding of the year. And if that meant Miranda had to do every single thing herself, had to check and double-check every detail a dozen times, then that's what she'd do. Ainsley, the youngest of Miranda's four siblings, would be the first to marry and it was important that her wedding be an especially memorable event for the entire family.

For as far back as she could remember, Miranda had looked forward to birthdays, holidays or any other occasion that brought her parents home...even though they never stayed for long. Charles and Linney Danville were always leaving for one faraway place or another. Miranda had lost count of the many goodbyes she'd waved to her parents as they left their ancestral home, Danfair, and their children, Matthew, Miranda, Andrew and Ainsley, in order to help someone less fortunate in some other corner of the earth. And, as the Danvilles had an abundance of riches—much of it channeled into the philanthropic Danville Foundation—almost everyone *was* less fortunate. Which meant there was always someplace—other than the cliffs of Newport, Rhode Island—where Charles and Linney were needed.

Miranda knew she was fortunate to have parents who believed that great wealth demanded great responsibility and who, from the start of their marriage, were committed to making the philanthropic work of the Foundation their mission in life. They traveled the world, bringing food, medicine and teams of workers to benefit the victims of war or famine, earthquakes or floods. Their humanitarian aid had helped so many, brought hope where none had existed, made such a difference in so many lives that Miranda couldn't begrudge her parents their choices, even if, on many occasions, she had wished for a more normal family life. One in which the parents were the primary caregivers instead of a series of nannies and an assortment of housekeeping staff.

The arrangement had made for an odd childhood for Miranda and her siblings—they weren't orphans, exactly, but they lacked the presence of a parent just the same. Their extended family consisted of one uncle—Edward, Charles's younger brother, Edward's wife, Aunt Ellora, and three cousins, Scott, Emily and Claire. No one seemed to think any crisis could arise that Uncle Edward couldn't handle, at least until Charles and Linney could make it home. And, as far as Miranda knew, it had never occurred to either Charles or Linney that their children weren't perfectly fine—even, perhaps, better off—inside the safe walls of Danfair than they would be under the roof of their uncle and aunt.

So, for much of the time, the four Danville children had been left to their own devices…watched over by strangers who kept them safe and provided for their basic needs, but comforted and cared for mainly by one another. Since there had been no one else to do it, Miranda had taken on Linney's role as mother to Matt, Andrew and Ainsley. She'd handled the little and large details of their lives. She'd learned to make lists. She'd learned to be organized. She'd learned to plan ahead. In the back of her mind, she'd always expected that one day there'd be an end to it, a point at which her parents would come home and take over the daily responsibilities of the children they'd brought into the world and she'd be free to live her own life without bearing—however cheerfully—the responsibility of caring for someone else's children. But that hadn't happened.

Until now.

Now that she, Matt, Andrew and Ainsley were all officially adults.

Now that Ainsley was going to be married.

For Miranda, the wedding represented a demarcation, a distinct separation between past and present. It was the signal for change, the moment she would feel free of the responsibility of caring for someone else's children. She didn't know why Ainsley's marriage seemed like such a milestone to her or why she felt such an obligation to make the wedding as grand and wonderful as possible.

Maybe it had to do with the fact that she was twenty-nine, closing in on thirty, and beginning to think that life was passing her by while she took care of running Danfair and smoothing the bumps for her siblings and her parents. Maybe it had to do with the fact that Charles and Linney were coming home, which was always cause for celebration. Their time at Danfair had always been limited and so their presence had become an event in itself, enough reason to celebrate. For them to return for their youngest child's wedding…well, in Miranda's opinion, that rated an extra-special effort.

And celebrations, as Miranda well knew, took careful planning.

A concept that wouldn't occur to Ainsley. She had never been particularly interested in thinking too far ahead. She went through life like a sunbeam, unconcerned about the details. And now that she was in love… Well, Miranda knew the task of putting together the wedding would fall largely to her. Somehow the details of her family's lives always fell to her. Always had. In one way or another, they probably always would.

"October?" Erica Hibbard, Miranda's best friend and most reliable commiserator, looked up from perusing the buffet table, a frown creasing her forehead, a cherry tomato speared on her fork. "But that's only three months away. It's impossible to put together a decent dinner party in that length of time, much less a wedding."

"Try telling that to Ainsley." Miranda searched the appetizers for something more appealing than a celery stick, but the trays were pretty well picked over already. There would, she decided, be no shortage of vegetables at Ainsley's wedding. "She and Ivan don't want to wait. They've chosen Halloween as their wedding date and, so far, I haven't been able to persuade them to postpone their nuptials by so much as a week, much less until next year. No matter what argument I make, neither of them will budge."

"But didn't your parents just leave for Sierra Leone? Will they even be back before October?"

"They'll be home in time for the wedding," she said, not allowing the sentence to end with a sigh, although she knew Erica would have been very understanding. "Mother told me she knew Baby would be a beautiful bride no matter what the date or the weather. And she trusts me—can you believe she said that?—to help Ainsley put together a lovely wedding."

"Have you tried talking to Ivan? Maybe he has some sense about the practicalities and can persuade Ainsley to postpone the wedding. Or at least, to choose a date other than Halloween."

Miranda had to fight the urge to roll her eyes. "Are you kidding? Since they got engaged, he's been even less sensible than she is."

"But he's a doctor…and he just started his job at the new pediatric-research center."

Lifting an expressive "you-think-I-don't-know-this?" eyebrow at her friend, Miranda turned back to the depleted appetizer trays. "Nothing will get done if I don't do it," she said. "You know that as well as I do. Their wedding could be worse than Scott's and they wouldn't even notice." Deciding against the cherry tomatoes—potentially too messy—she followed Erica along the curve of the buffet table, picking up only two carrot sticks and a tiny flat-looking quiche to place beside the solitary celery stick, with some horrible-looking cheese mixture spread over the top on her plate. "That's the problem when someone as flighty as my sister falls in love with a man who's sunny side is always up. Practicality gets smudged in the glow of their rose-colored glasses."

Erica nodded agreement and ruthlessly stabbed

several pineapple chunks in succession, nabbing the fruit just ahead of a solid-looking woman who was wielding a skewer from the opposite side of the table. "You'll have to handle everything," Erica agreed with sympathy. "And on such short notice you'll never get Amy Ellen Vanderley. She's always booked well in advance. Suzanne Sinclair told me that Millicent Richards has already put her daughter's name on Amy Ellen's client list and that child isn't even out of braces yet."

"I'm not going to hire a wedding planner," Miranda said, making the decision on the spot. "I'm going to do it myself."

Erica stopped in midcapture of a cocktail sausage—*Imagine! Cocktail sausages served at a Danville wedding. There would be no such hors d'oeuvre at Ainsley's wedding. Period. No discussion.*—losing the sausage to the skewer by a quarter inch. "Miranda!" she said. "You can't do it without a professional planner. There's not enough time. Even you can't work miracles."

Actually, Miranda thought she could come close…if she had enough time to make the appropriate lists, hire appropriate help and attend to the details of coordinating all the little items that made up a "miracle." "I can do better than this—" she gestured broadly at the scanty amounts of food

"—in my sleep. And honestly, how hard can it be to plan a wedding?"

Erica's round pixyish face crimped with worry. "*Three months,* Miranda. Think how *stressed* you'll be."

Miranda didn't think she would be that stressed. She loved a challenge, loved being busy, loved proving she *could* do what others said couldn't be done. "Stressed is desserts spelled backward, you know," Miranda said, apropos of nothing. "I'll be fine."

"But what about the election?" Erica pressed, moving on down the line to trays that still held a few tidbits of smoked salmon, boiled shrimp and some sort of pâté. "Don't you need to do at least some campaigning to keep your city council seat?"

Miranda laughed. "The only person in my ward to file against me is Beatrice Combs and everyone knows her only reason for doing it is so she can fuss about the tourists. No one will vote for her. A sitting councillor hasn't lost a reelection bid in years. I'm not worried." Picking up the tongs, she captured a skimpy portion of shrimp and dropped it onto her plate. "I have several private landscape-design projects under construction and the one large project still on my desk is an update of the Foundation's Peace Garden. But my busiest schedule is always late winter, early spring, when people start thinking about new landscaping. I have plenty of time now to plan the wedding.''

''That's very optimistic of you.''

''No, simply realistic.'' She leaned over the table, reaching with the tongs to secure a tasty-looking but rather soggy chunk of the salmon. ''Ainsley is getting married in October whether I'm up to my ears in work or just sitting around twiddling my thumbs. I *have* to plan the wedding, Erica, or it will turn out worse than this one.'' She gestured to encompass the buffet tables again to emphasize her point, but the tongs made a sudden metallic *clank* as they connected with an obstacle of similar size and Miranda looked up just in time to see the chunk of smoked salmon fly through the air and splatter across a crisp white shirtfront.

Embarrassed beyond belief, she sent her gaze up the lines of a funky blue-and-yellow-print tie, past a solid, honest-seeming chin at the base of a charmingly handsome face. A pair of friendly, if somewhat startled, brown eyes met hers and a response as sweet as a hug wrapped around her, followed almost instantly by a quicksilver stab of attraction. He *was* attractive and the air felt suddenly charged with awareness, making Miranda almost grateful for the swift and distracting infusion of self-consciousness that warmed her cheeks. ''Oh,'' she said, her voice a breathy rush that couldn't all be blamed on embarrassment. "I am sooooo sorry!"

His smile curved wryly as he plucked the salmon from where it clung tenaciously, and very messily, to his chest, and dropped it onto his plate. Then he licked his fingers. "In other circumstances, I might be a little upset that my shirt's messed up," he said, his voice unoffended and rich with humor. "But considering how hungry I am, I think I'll just thank you for sharing and ask you to toss over that celery stick."

She laughed. Breathily conscious of how flirtatious, how *not* like herself she sounded. "Really," she said, forcing her voice to a more normal pitch. "I'm very sorry. I don't know how that happened."

"Our tongs collided," he said. "It was fate."

Fate. He believed it was fate. The thought danced through her mind like fairy dust while she stood there smiling, feeling a loopy impulse to giggle. Except she never giggled, didn't even know how. "I don't believe in fate," she said, gathering some normalcy. "But I do believe in the power of club soda, and if I were you, I'd get some on that shirt before the stain sets."

He glanced down, then brought his whiskey-brown eyes back to hers, puzzled, interested. "Club soda, huh?"

"That's what I'd use," she began. "Unless I had…"

"Nate! You old son of a gun! I thought it was you!"

Miranda's advice trailed away, overpowered by the robust greeting of a slight, middle-aged man with more smile than hair, who'd cut into the line with the clear intent of intercepting the man she'd just been talking with. Nate. His name was Nate.

"I'd heard you were back in Newport, but I thought it was probably only a rumor," the man said, one hand clasping Nate's in a handshake, the other grasping his elbow in a good-buddy squeeze. "I'm glad to see you're not holed up in that big house, waiting for some of the old gang to come and coax you out. We're not any of us the party animals we used to be, you know. Though I don't suppose you're the good-time Charlie you used to be, either."

"Mark." Nate grinned and returned the handshake with gusto. "It's great to see you. I've been home about a month now. Trying to get settled. You know how that goes."

"Sure do," Mark agreed amiably, nodding as if he did indeed know. Then his expression sobered. "Deb and I were really sorry to hear about Angie. We just couldn't believe it. There's nothing to say except I sure wish it hadn't happened."

"Me, too." Nate's expression was somber for a passing moment, but then his smile returned. "Maybe we can all get together. Recap some of our college adventures. Do you ever see Dalton Hughes? Is he still around here? And Jenny Oles? What about her?"

Mark laughed. "I always thought you had a thing for Jenny. Before Angie came along, anyway. Well, the last I heard, Jen's in Boston. Married to a…"

"Miranda?" Erica, two steps down the buffet line, gestured for attention. "You're holding up the line," she said, loud enough to be heard, quietly enough not to be overheard. "And I think they're bringing out the wedding cake. Maybe we can at least get a piece of that before it's gone."

Miranda moved forward, forcing herself not to look back at the man whose name was Nate. He should do something about that stain, she thought. He really should.

NATE WATCHED HER walk away, admiring the graceful swing of her hips, regretting the interruption, wondering if he even knew how to talk to women anymore. As a single guy, that is. At forty-four, he'd been married nearly half his life, and spending almost twenty years with the same woman—while certainly a good experience—didn't exactly keep the old dating skills honed and razor sharp. But then he'd never expected he'd *want* to date again.

Angie had told him he would, had several times expressed her opinion that he shouldn't wait too long to start, either, as it would probably take a while to find a woman willing to take on a widower with four children. She'd also instructed the kids to be nice to any woman who was crazy enough to go out with him more than once.

That was Angie. Smoothing out the future her family faced without her, striking out at the curve-ball life had tossed to her.

"She's candy for the old eyes, that's for sure." Mark's gaze followed Nate's, lingering on the slender blonde as she left the buffet line and disappeared into another room. "If I were a few years younger and slightly less married, I'd be tempted to give that one the old Lambda Delta rush."

Nate frowned, bringing his attention back to Mark. "Watch it there, buddy. You make it sound as if we're already over the hill. Unless you've been packing in a lot more birthdays than I have, we're both still young, with plenty of good years ahead of us."

Mark looked at him sadly. "We're on the shady side of forty, Nate. A couple more birthdays and we'll be getting our membership cards from the AARP."

The American Association for Retired Persons? The official You-Are-Old *membership card?* Nate wasn't even forty-five yet. Not until December, which was nearly six months away and he certainly didn't feel that old, even if he was, technically, retired. "Whatever happened to 'you're only as old as you feel?'"

"Only old people say things like that." Mark shook his head, as if there were only rocking chairs and dentures ahead for them. "I'm afraid we're past the age of innocence, my friend. Women like Miranda Danville see guys like us—if they even look at us at all—as father figures. Or worse, as dirty old men."

"Now, wait a minute," Nate started to protest those equally unflattering images, but suddenly the name registered and he blinked in surprise. "Miranda Danville?" He repeated, looking toward the spot where he'd seen her last. "*That* was Miranda Danville?"

"The one and only."

"But she used to date my kid brother."

"There ya go," Mark said, as if that proved his point.

And maybe it did, since Nate remembered Miranda as a long-legged coltish teenager. Which he supposed had been exactly what she was at the time. How long ago had it been? Fourteen, fifteen years?

And why he remembered this one girl—out of all the girls Nick had dated—was a mystery. Maybe because Miranda had been beautiful even then. Or maybe he just remembered that summer visit so well because it had been the first time he and Angie had brought the babies home to meet their grandmother and uncle. Will and Cate were thirteen now, so it had been thirteen years. Jeez, how fast the time had gone.

"I can't get over running into you like this," Mark said, clapping him on the shoulder. "It's really great to see you looking so well, Nate. How long will you be home this time? Or is the real question how long Uncle Sam can run the country without you?"

"He's been running it without me since May." Nate eyed the buffet table again. "I'm a civilian again."

"What?" Mark's eyes widened with envy and surprise. "Don't tell me you're retired!"

Nate nodded as he used a spoon to scoop some sort of rice mixture onto his plate. "Retired."

"Wow. Wish I could figure out a way to do that. Of course, I should have followed your example and taken the military route. Twenty years in the air force and here you are."

"Twenty-two years and, yes, here I am." Nate wasn't sure where, exactly, *here* was. But here he was, nonetheless. "Listen, it's great seeing you, too. But I probably should get on through this line before the backup causes a food fight."

"Not enough food for that. Don't know what happened. It isn't like the Danvilles to skimp on the buffet. Maybe they didn't expect such a crowd. You may not have heard that the bride left Scott at the altar last time they tried this. She ran off with some guy in a Batmobile. The family should have known everyone would turn out to see what would happen this time. Why, even you're here." Mark laughed. "But seriously, now that you're back, we're not going to let you be a stranger. Deb's around here somewhere. I know she'll want to say hello. Why don't I find her and we'll—"

There was a long drumroll, picked up from outside where the musicians were stationed and carried throughout the house by the sound system. Nate felt a moment's relief that it overpowered whatever plans Mark had been about to make. It wasn't that Nate was averse to seeing old friends and renewing old friendships. He'd been looking forward to it, in fact, knew it would be easier to make a life here, where he had roots, a history.

Angie had always planned for them to return to Rhode Island when he retired from the air force. No matter where in the world they'd been stationed, she'd worked hard to maintain the relationships they'd left behind. It was important, she'd said, that their children have a sense of home, a place where they felt they belonged. Now, especially, Nate saw the wisdom in that. The kids had never lived in Newport, had only visited from time to time, but already they were settling in as if they'd never lived anywhere else. Angie had been right about that, too…yet another example of her foresight. Nate was consistently surprised to realize just how well she'd prepared them to go on without her.

The drumroll faded and a deep voice announced, "The bride and groom will be cutting the wedding cake out on the east veranda in a few minutes. After the toasts, Scott and Molly will share their first dance as husband and wife. Guests are encouraged to make their way to the veranda now. That's the *east* veranda. Dancing will be outdoors near the pergola."

In the general hubbub that followed the announcement, Mark gave Nate a see-you-later clap on the shoulder and disappeared into the crowd, presumably in search of Deb. Nate left the buffet line, too, and wandered back to the table where his date was waiting. "They're going to cut the cake," he said as he slipped into the chair beside her and placed the plate of food on the table. "Do you want to go to the east veranda and watch?"

Charleigh Shepard was one of those women who

improved with age, the years mellowing the taut angles of her elongated face and settling easily into the spareness of her body. At forty, she had looked older, but at seventy-three she had an agelessness that was both confident and benignly charming. Nate had never been able to decide if the softness had developed over the years as a natural evolution of her life experiences or if she'd cultivated the change within herself. He only knew she was his mother and that she was beautiful. Even when she allowed herself to frown…as she was doing now. "I watched the wedding," she said. "Isn't that enough?"

He laughed. "Now, Mother, you're the one who wanted to come to this wedding. If you'll recall, I suggested it would be more fun to stay home and play poker."

She had a way of looking at him that said more than he wanted to hear about whatever topic she wasn't going to discuss. It was a trick he tried on a regular basis with his own children. To no effect, unless he counted the times they laughed hysterically while imitating *Dad-trying-to-give-us-the-look*. "Okay," he said now, giving in without her having to say a word. "I know I said I wanted to plunge right into the social scene. And I do. I just wanted another month to anticipate it."

"You've had a month," she replied tartly. "And

the only thing you've done is putter around the house and aggravate the children. And me.''

''That's not true. The kids always act that way. So do you, for that matter. And I've been fixing up the house and...*and*...'' He warmed to his defense. ''I've bought a building near the harbor that I'm going to renovate into a coffee bar. *And* I signed up to run for a seat on the city council. If that's not *plunging* into life in the community, I don't know what is.''

Charleigh sniffed, unimpressed. ''At the rate your campaign is progressing, Nathaniel, even I won't vote for you. For heaven's sake, look around. Here you are at a wedding, surrounded by potential supporters, and if you've shaken one hand, I'll eat my hat.''

''It would probably taste better than that rice,'' he said. ''And on the contrary, I have shaken hands. With Mark Olivant. Over by the buffet table. You remember Mark?''

''Of course I remember Mark. I also remember that he lives in Jamestown, not in Newport, not in our ward, and he will not be voting in our city elections in November.''

Nate frowned, undaunted by his mother's chiding. ''Jamestown, huh? Well, I won't be shaking *his* hand again. Can't waste perfectly good handshakes on nonvoters.''

Charleigh's smile was affectionate, if slightly reluctant. "It's good to have you home, son. Nicky isn't quite the source of entertainment you've always been."

"That's because he pops in and out as if the house had a revolving door, never giving even ten minutes' alert that he's coming home and barely five minutes' warning that he's leaving again. If he'd spent the last twenty-five years only visiting you once or twice a year, you'd probably find him much more entertaining, too."

"I'm thinking of moving to Florida," she announced evenly as if she were merely musing on what the weather would be tomorrow. "Your aunt Tilda loves it there. She's been begging me to buy a place near hers and I've just about decided to go down next month and check it out."

This was new. And unsettling. "I offered to get a place of our own, Mother. I can still do that."

She smiled softly, a little sadly, and patted his hand. "The house has been too empty for too long. It's right that you and your children should have it. Lord knows, Nicky would sell it if he got half a chance. Revolving door notwithstanding."

Nate acknowledged that with a rueful grin. "Or worse…raze it and build some architectural nightmare in its place."

"Angie and I talked about this, Nathaniel. We

agreed that the children need the security of living in the home in which you grew up. What they don't need is a grandmother trying to fill their mother's role…and you know I'd try to do that. I can't help myself.''

''That's not going to happen,'' Nate said, wanting to believe it. ''No one will ever take Angie's place. Or her role in the children's lives.''

''Maybe not for Will and Cate. But the little ones? Kali and Kori are barely seven. They're still forming…and as much as I hate to say this, Nate, it's clear to me that you're not entirely comfortable with being a single parent.''

''No, I'm not,'' he agreed, stung not so much by the truth of that as by the awareness that she knew it. ''It's going to take a while to be *entirely* comfortable with anything. If it's even possible. Angie's only been gone a year.''

''And she was dying for three years before that. You've grieved for her, Nate. Your children have grieved. Now it's time for you to start out as you mean to go on. By plunging into life. For the children's sake if not for your own.''

He thrummed his fingertips on the table, heard voices and laughter coming from the east terrace where the cake cutting must be commencing. ''You sound like Angie,'' he said finally. Because, really, there wasn't anything else to say. His mother was right. Angie had known he'd be scared out of his wits at the idea of raising their children to adulthood without her. It wasn't that he thought he was a *bad* father. On occasion, he was positive he'd been a damn good one. So far, anyway. But he'd depended on Angie to smooth any rough edges, to balance his tendency to issue orders, as he had been accustomed to doing in the military. He'd counted on her to be around to share the responsibility with him. He'd never in a million years thought he'd have to bear it alone. Angie had known all that, just as she'd understood, too, that he'd be tempted to allow his mother to take on some of that responsibility if she offered.

"She hoped you'd remarry, Nate. You know that."

"Yes, I do. She probably figured I'd totally mess up the kids if left to my own devices. But, personally, I think she was wrong about that."

Charleigh smiled. "I think so, too. But I did promise her I'd make certain you got into the social swing and stayed there. So let's go see if the wedding cake looks better than this." She nodded at the untouched food on the plate. "And then I'll have some wine and watch you dance."

He was already on his feet, extending a hand to help her up…because she'd raised him to be a gentleman. Not because she needed any help. She was a spry seventy-three and could probably dance circles around him still. "I wasn't planning on doing any dancing."

"Nonsense," she stated succinctly, rising easily and taking his arm. "You can ask some lovely young woman to dance, or if you prefer, I can do it for you."

"Angie put you up to this, didn't she?"

"I do have an occasional idea of my own, but Angie did mention, several times in conversation, that you're a wonderful dancer and shouldn't be allowed to pretend otherwise."

"How about I pretend I was adopted?"

"Too late, I'm afraid. You'll just have to face your fear of rejection and ask someone to dance. It won't kill you."

"Oh, nicely put, Mother." He guided her toward the terrace doors and the sounds of the orchestra playing an overblown version of "The Way You Look Tonight." "So…are you going to tell me who you want me to ask or do I have to go through a painful process of elimination?"

"I saw that lovely Miranda Danville talking to you across the buffet line. Why don't you ask her?"

"She used to date Nicky."

"Yes, but I think we should forgive her that lapse. She was very young then."

"And I was married and a new father."

"And now you're not." Charleigh nodded, decision made. "You'll ask Miranda. After we've tested the cake and had some wine."

The idea of dancing with Miranda was undeniably appealing. Also a trifle intimidating. She was beautiful. Not that dogs howled maniacally at his approach, but he knew his face was more character actor than soap opera star. And Miranda was also young. Not that he was *old,* but Mark had just told him that women like her looked at men like him as…well, *older.* Not that age mattered. Angie would be the first to point that out if she were here. Which, of course, she wasn't.

Which brought him right back to the question of how to ask a young and beautiful woman to dance.

He was still pondering the *how* of it when his mother eventually pushed away her cake plate, dotted her mouth with a napkin and lifted her eyebrows expectantly.

"More cake?" he asked hopefully.

Her smile told him the grace period was over even as her attention moved past him and up. "Why, Miranda," she said graciously, "how lovely to see you."

A long, slow tingle slid the length of his spine as he pushed back from the table and stood, turning to see the woman, who'd occupied most of his thoughts since she'd hit him in the chest with her salmon, standing at his elbow, a bottle of club soda clutched in her hand.

"You remember my son Nathaniel?" Charleigh said.

"Oh…yes, of course," Miranda answered, clearly *not* remembering until that very second. "Nate."

"I'm Nicky's older brother." He couldn't believe he'd said the O word first thing. *Way to go, Nate.* "But I hope you won't hold that against me."

She smiled a little uncertainly. "I, uh…no. No, I always rather liked Nick. Although I haven't seen him in some time. A long time, actually." Her smile hesitated, turned from him to his mother. "How *is* Nick?" she asked as if she thought, perhaps, she ought to ask.

"Still wildly attractive and unattractively wild. From a mother's standpoint, anyway."

"Oh." Miranda's lovely eyes—blue with an intriguing touch of gold—flickered to Nate's, returned to Charleigh. "I see his picture on the newsstands occasionally."

Charleigh smiled, proud of her youngest child despite his shortcomings. "He's very popular at *Soap Opera Digest.*"

Mainly because his private life was as full of bizarre intrigues as his alter ego's, Daxson Darck, on

Sunset Beach. But Nate didn't feel the need to point that out. Nor did his mother.

Miranda hesitated, then turned to Nate. "I got some club soda," she said, offering him the bottle. "For your shirt."

Nate took the bottle from her hand with no intent of touching her except in the most casual way. But she had a grip on the club soda, almost as if she was reluctant to let it go, and his fingers lingered for a moment on hers. The spark of recognition flared, instantaneous and erotic. And he pulled back from the exchange almost as quickly as she.

"It's so interesting that you should walk up just now, Miranda," Charleigh was saying with a conversational smile. "Because Nate was just talking about you."

"He was?"

A soft touch of color bloomed on her cheeks and despite every effort to stay unaffected, Nate was charmed to the core. She had felt it, too, that moment of awareness. It might have been a long time since he'd shared that first recognition of electric attraction, but it wasn't the sort of thing a man forgot.

"Was he explaining how I ruined his shirt? I still can't believe that happened."

"Our tongs collided," Nate informed his mother,

pointing to the stain, which until that minute he'd forgotten was there. "It was fate."

Charleigh glanced at his shirtfront. "Fate?"

"I was hungry. She was tossing salmon."

"How serendipitous." Charleigh's smile turned to Miranda. "No, actually he was wondering aloud if I thought you might dance with him. If he asked. I was just telling him I was sure you would when, suddenly, here you are."

Miranda looked surprised, but she didn't seem appalled by the thought of dancing with him. Nate considered that a positive sign. Below the drape of the tablecloth, his mother's foot nudged his. "Miranda," he asked obediently, "would you like to dance?"

"Um, sure," she replied doubtfully, her gaze flickering to his chest, then back to his face. "Unless you'd rather get some club soda on that stain."

"Probably best to let the dry cleaners treat it," Charleigh said, apparently believing he'd take any excuse to get out of dancing.

But even mothers were wrong on occasion. And although he might be on the shady side of forty, he was a long way from passing up the opportunity to hold a beautiful woman in his arms. "The club soda will wait for me," he said. "The music won't."

He took her hand, seeking, and finding, that shiver of electric response, and led her to the dance floor, where he drew her into his arms. The song was as soft as the night air around them. And Nate felt like a young man at his first formal dance. Expectant. Excited. Uncertain.

"I hope you don't mind," he said. "It's been quite a while since I was in this position."

She held herself rather stiffly, not exactly *melting* against him, but she looked up at that and smiled. And his heart skipped a beat. Maybe he *was* too old for this. "What position?" she asked. "Dancing?"

"Having my mother kick me in the instep until I asked you to dance. She thinks I'm backward with women."

Miranda's eyebrow arched prettily. "And are you?"

"I don't know. I never thought so before."

"Before she kicked you?"

He grinned. "Sometime around then, yes." Relaxing into the rhythm of the music, he tried to draw Miranda closer, but she resisted, one palm pressed rather solidly against his chest. He didn't insist, of course, but wondered if maybe she hadn't wanted to dance with him. Maybe Mark had been right and women like Miranda viewed men over forty with suspicion. Or distaste.

But he knew he hadn't imagined the attraction. Or the subtle blush still lingering in her cheeks. He felt the attraction now, was reasonably sure she was feeling it, too. And she didn't seem the type to be nervous about dancing with a man, even if he wasn't exactly the Prince Charming she might have had in mind.

On the other hand…there was her palm maintaining a curious, if not completely unreasonable, distance between them.

And then it hit him.

The stain on his shirt bothered her. She either didn't want to come into contact with it or she felt afraid of making it worse if she did. He had to restrain a ridiculous grin from eating up his entire face. Either reason was perfectly acceptable to him as utterly, unexpectedly charming. She was *worried* about the stupid stain and it was all she could do to be out here dancing, instead of inside, at one sink or another, scrubbing salmon juice out of his shirt.

He stopped in midstep. "I'm sorry," he said, taking her hand and turning toward the house. "But I can't concentrate on anything except getting that club soda on this shirt."

Her relief was instant and companionable. "I was thinking the same thing. The longer it sets, the harder it will be to get out."

"My thoughts exactly," he replied, intrigued by the warmth in her hand and completely captivated by the smile in her eyes.

Chapter Two

Nate snapped the front pages of the *Providence Journal* to a comfortable reading position and settled in to enjoy his morning coffee with the news. He got through the headlines and one paragraph of the lead article before getting up to top off the coffee and check the fridge for orange juice. Back to the table, he reread the paragraph, then decided a little toast would go well with the juice and tide him over until breakfast. Once the bread was in the toaster, he stood, somewhat impatiently, and waited for it to brown. He wondered what Miranda Danville was having for breakfast or if she ate breakfast at all. Lots of girls didn't.

Not that Miranda was a girl.

Oh, no. She was a woman. Definitely. He could still feel the soft, very womanly curve of her in his arms.

Not that she'd really been in his arms.

The dance hadn't lasted a minute. But the memory of her serious, somber expression as she'd watched him dab club soda onto his shirt stayed with him. She'd been so intent on the stain, so concerned about her part in ruining his shirt, that he wasn't even startled when she'd grabbed the towel from his inept hands and worked diligently on blotting the stain herself.

Not that he hadn't been startled.

The sheer force of the attraction that had cut through him at her touch was enough to scare any man. Any man with good sense, that is.

Not that standing here thinking about her like this showed particularly good sense.

She was too young for him. Or more aptly, he was too old for her. He was the father of two thirteen-year-olds and two seven-year-olds. He'd been several years into his career before she was out of braces. He'd been married since she was in grade school. If he were going to date—and he wasn't sure as yet that he was ready—it ought to be with someone closer to his age and experience. A widow, maybe. A single mother. Someone who understood the intricacies of family life, the challenges of parenting. That couldn't happen with someone like Miranda.

Not that it *couldn't* happen. But it didn't seem very likely.

Why was he even thinking about her? The truth was, she couldn't be the least bit interested in dating someone with his experience. His *years and years* of experience.

Not that experience meant he had nothing to offer. He was, after all, a hell of a nice guy. Angie had told him that repeatedly and he had no reason to believe she'd lied about it. He had means, too—a decent retirement income on top of the substantial wealth he'd inherited by virtue of being born his father's son. He had a Juris Doctorate, too, so he could practice law again, if he wanted. That wasn't too shabby a list of qualifications, he thought, and then wondered why he was listing all he had to offer a woman when he'd already pretty much decided he wasn't even ready to date.

The encounter with Miranda Danville had spooked him, that was it. He hadn't expected to feel that sort of instantaneous, animal attraction, wouldn't have thought he *could* feel it again. He wasn't sure he even *wanted* to feel it. Attraction led to liking and liking led to intimacy and intimacy led to love and…well, loving someone again seemed like one hell of a commitment. It was one thing to think he might want to marry again someday but a whole other thing to realize love—and the inevitable possibility of losing that love—was part of the deal.

But he was getting way ahead of himself. Worrying about something so far-fetched seemed ridiculous. Well, not *that* far-fetched. His eyesight was still as keen as ever and he hadn't imagined the look of awareness in Miranda's lovely blue eyes. Nor had he invented the intriguing blush of color he'd seen on her pearly cheeks. The attraction he'd felt had been mutual. He knew that as well as he knew his name. It was the *what-came-next* that had him buffaloed.

The toast popped up, nutty brown and crisp, and he gingerly snatched it out and dropped it onto the counter as he searched through the cabinets for a plate. He wasn't exactly at home in the kitchen, even though he'd grown up in this house and ought, at least, to remember where Maggie kept the dishes. But he wasn't accustomed to fixing his own toast. Or being alone in the kitchen. His mother had left early, off on another of the day-long antique hunts she loved, dragging Maggie, the live-in housekeeper and cook, who was more friend than employee, more companion than help, along with her. The two women had waved a cheery goodbye to Nate, who had been intrigued by the novelty of a little Sunday-morning silence. With luck, Kali and Kori might sleep until he'd finished the paper. Will and Cate, being teenagers, invariably slept through the morning hours whenever possible.

Returning to the table with the toast, he took a

sip of coffee and picked up the newspaper again. The coffee had cooled and he should have buttered the toast before sitting down again, but he was determined to read the newspaper before the children invaded his solitude. Even if he did find it difficult to concentrate.

It was too damn quiet, that was the problem…and his mind was more interested in going over and over the few insignificant minutes he'd spent with Miranda Danville than in focusing on the world's myriad problems.

He needed noise, the shrill, rattling chaos his kids normally provided free of charge to keep his mind off an encounter that hadn't amounted to much of anything. Miranda was too young and too beautiful to find him of interest. Unless he could manage to get a particularly heinous stain on his clothing just before he met up with her again.

"Hi, Dad!"

His wish for distraction was granted, the silence scuttled as Kali did the bunny hop past his chair, her dark brown ponytails—doggy ears?—he never could keep those straight—bouncing. Or maybe this was Kori. Even after seven years of practice, he still sometimes had trouble telling them apart. If they stood perfectly still, shoulder to shoulder, right in front of him, he could do it in a snap. But when in motion, as they usually were, or when he saw one without the other—like now—well, it wasn't so easy. Since Angie died, they seemed to find comfort in looking as much alike as possible and Nate couldn't recall the last time he'd seen them dressed in anything except matching outfits. He probably ought to do something about that. Suggest they wear matching outfits in different colors, maybe. Or stand still more often.

"What's for breakfast?" She braced her feet on the black-and-white tile and tugged at the refrigerator door, opening it with a tremendous—mainly unnecessary—show of effort. "How 'bout we have your famous pancakes?"

Dad's famous pancakes was family code for going out to breakfast. Angie had made a joke about the fact that anytime she suggested he cook, he suggested they go out to eat. The kids loved to tease him, made up all kinds of fictitious stories about his ineptitude in all matters domestic. He'd always played along because it made them laugh and he'd never felt any particular need to apologize for not knowing how to do the things Angie did so well. But suddenly he felt inadequate, as if his children might have to suffer through years on a psychiatrist's couch because he didn't know how to make pancakes. "I can fix you some toast," he offered, taking a bite out of his own. "Pretty tasty."

Kali—he was almost positive it was Kali and not

Kori—looked at him with eyes like his own, but set into her mother's heart-shaped face, with a handful of Angie's freckles scattered across her pert little nose. "No, thank you," she said, and turned back to studying the contents of the fridge. "Can I have a Popsicle, please?"

He knew sugar was probably the worst thing for a seven-year-old at this time of day. Or later, for that matter. On the other hand, she had said please. "Sure," he answered, not seeing the harm. "Why not?"

Her smile, too, reminded him of Angie, in all its crinkly cuteness. But then, except for their eyes, his little daughters were their mother made over. Dark, brown hair, rusty freckles, sassy attitude, all born in them as if Mother Nature had wanted to ensure Angie wouldn't be forgotten.

As if that were ever a possibility.

He watched Angie's child assess the problem of retrieving the requested Popsicle. Chin up, she reached for the handle of the side-by-side freezer, approaching it as if she'd need eighty pounds of heft in order to pry it open. Nate was tempted to get up to help, but knew from experience she'd rather do it on her own. The door popped open easily, obviously a pleasant surprise, and she smiled while plunging her hand into the box of Popsicles and coming out with the treat successfully in her grasp.

She closed the freezer door with her hip and bounced happily over to the table, where she pulled out a chair and sat down, apparently unconcerned about having left the refrigerator door wide-open.

He got up and closed it, warming up his coffee— again—before returning to his place at the table. He smiled across at her as she licked the orange ice and she smiled back. There was something different about her this morning. Her hair was pulled into two neat ponytails—doggy ears, he decided, was what Angie had called that particular hairstyle—which were each tied with two overlapping ribbons, one blue, one yellow. She was dressed in yellow shorts and a blue-and-yellow-striped T-shirt. A matching outfit. Hmm. "You look nice this morning," he commented, wondering how she'd gotten her hair so neat.

"Thanks," she said, her mouth full of Popsicle. "Cate did it for me. She's doing Kori's now."

Aha. This *was* Kali. He should have trusted his instincts. But then the oddity of what she'd said registered. "*Cate* fixed your hair? This morning?"

Kali nodded, apparently seeing nothing unusual in the idea that her sister was up before…he glanced at the clock on the kitchen wall…nine-thirty—a.m.

"Did you wake her up?" he asked.

"Nooooo." Kali stretched out the word, turning

it into an *I'm-not-stupid, Dad* statement. "She's got a date."

"Oh," Nate said, then frowned. "She isn't old enough to date."

Kali shrugged and Kori came into the kitchen, identical to her twin in every detail, right down to the coordinating ribbons in her hair. Nate decided he would definitely give some thought to suggestions he could make about emphasizing their individuality. "Hey," she said. "Where'd you get a Popsicle?"

"From the freezer."

Kori looked expectantly at Nate. "She's got a Popsicle."

"He said I could have it." Kali gave the ice a smug swipe with her tongue.

"Dad!" Kori's tone was egregiously offended. "How come she gets a Popsicle?"

"Because she asked?" Nate suggested, his mood perked by the level of distraction now percolating in the room.

"Can I have one?"

"Yes, you may have one."

Kori's smile flashed like neon and he was suddenly aware of a strange mix of color on her teeth. "What's wrong with your teeth?" he asked, leaning forward for a better look.

"Don't worry, Pops," she said, sounding a lot

like her older sister. "It's just wax. Doesn't it look like I have braces on?"

Before he could comment that it looked like just what it was—thin strips of green and pink orthodontic wax stuck across her front teeth—Cate walked in. She'd gotten tall over the last few months, and looked older even than she had yesterday. That could, of course, be the punk-funk style she'd been perfecting over the past couple of years. Her hair—today—was cranberry red with banana and blueberry streaks. At least she was sticking with healthy-fruit colors, he thought. She had a ring—fake, thankfully, as Angie had established a firm rule about no permanent holes in places where nature hadn't seen fit to put one in the first place—clipped on one eyebrow and a silver stud, magnetically attached—he knew because he'd insisted she show him—at her navel. He would have preferred that the navel jewelry wasn't visible, but at least her fringed crop top covered all of her except a three-inch band of skin at her waist.

Nate didn't like her showing any skin, but Angie had warned him not to fuss about the way the kids dressed. She'd told him fashion was a subjective statement and he did not want to set himself up as the arbiter of what they wore. That, she'd told him, would result in endless, futile arguments over what was relatively unimportant. They were great kids, good students who had to wear school uniforms for the nine months they were in class, and should be allowed to dress the way they wanted during the summers. With, of course, a few nonnegotiable rules. No low-cut necklines. No see-through clothing unless something opaque was worn underneath. No piercings. No tattoos. No shorts or skirt lengths higher than midthigh. No more than three inches of midriff showing at any time. This morning, Cate met the three-inch rule and so Nate bit his tongue and gave her a smile. "Good morning, Sunshine," he greeted her.

"Good morning, Dad." She came straight over, looped her arms around his neck and kissed him on the cheek. A diversionary action, probably. But it worked.

"What got you up and going so early this morning?"

She moved to the refrigerator, sweeping the Popsicle twins with a glance, which changed her direction, sending her to the sink where she wet one corner of a towel and returned to the table to wipe identical Popsicle-streaked mouths. "Is that, like, all you could find for breakfast?" she asked, her tone suggesting someone should have been paying more attention. "Don't you want, like, some cereal or something?"

Nate felt a sharp stab of guilt for her concern,

knew Angie would never forgive him if he let Cate take on the maternal role in the family. The trouble was, he didn't quite know how to stop her. Cate was a force unto herself, and despite her punk-rock style and the way she inserted *like* into practically every sentence, she was something of an old-fashioned girl. "I'll get it, Dad," she said when he made a move to rise. "You can finish your paper. They're, like, old enough to fix their own breakfast."

"Kali mentioned you had a date," he said, rising to fetch the cereal despite her protest, hoping to save her from doing it. But she was, of course, a step ahead of him and already had the cereal box in her hand. Which meant he could, at least, get the bowls. "Funny thing is, I don't remember your thirtieth birthday, and I'm pretty sure I said you weren't allowed to date before then."

She rolled her blue-green eyes, his mother's eyes, a striking combination with her brightly colored hair. "I'm going with Ariel and her mom to the mall, Dad. I told you that, like, yesterday."

He tried to remember, but a lot had happened since yesterday, and meeting Miranda seemed to have burned up a whole bunch of his memory cells. "You did?"

She lifted her eyebrows, resembling for a moment a badly colorized version of Angie. "Like, duh," she said.

He set the cereal bowls on the table in front of the twins, who ignored both bowls and cereal box in favor of their frozen Sugar Pops, and resumed his seat. He was trying to phrase a courteous but firm objection to Cate's attitude and her, *like*, plans, when Will came in, looking like something the cat had dragged out of the trash. If his twin sister's style was punk, Will's was grunge. His jeans were loose and baggy and Nate thought his son must have somehow outwitted gravity just to keep them from falling around his ankles. He had on a shirt that even a vagrant would have wanted to give away and his hair—although untouched by the wild witches of fruity colors—stuck up in odd peaks and valleys and appeared for all the world as if he'd stuck his finger into a light socket just before coming downstairs.

"Morning," he mumbled, because lately his voice squeaked more often than not and he'd taken to covering the embarrassing unevenness by barely moving his lips.

"Want a Popsicle, Will?"

Kori and Kali adored their big brother, despite his appearance, and their affection spilled out in big smiles. Nate noted the orthodontic wax—Kali had some on her teeth, too—was now a brownish color, stained by the orange pops.

"Yeah." Kori seconded Kali's invitation. "Dad said we could eat Popsicles for breakfast."

Will frowned and put a hand to his forehead, possibly shading his eyes from the wattage of their smiles. "What have you got on your teeth?" he wanted to know.

"Fake braces," Kori announced proudly.

"Cate helped us put them on," said Kali. "Don't they look real? Just like yours and Cate's."

"That's bogus," Will replied. Which could have meant great or awful. Nate didn't really care to know which.

Folding the paper into thirds, he laid it on the table and surveyed his children. Maybe he'd been too quick to wish away the morning quiet.

"Well," he said cheerfully, "you're all up remarkably early this morning. Guess you're excited about our plans for today, huh?"

"Huh?" Will looked at Nate as if he were a talking frog.

"What plans?" Cate asked, obviously horrified at the idea of a family outing.

"Are we going somewhere?" Kori asked as she tried to catch several fast-moving drips of Popsicle.

"If you'll recall," Nate said, "I told you guys I'd take you downtown this afternoon and show you the building we're going to renovate for our coffeehouse. Since you're all up and dressed already, I'll take you out for brunch on the way."

Cate and Will exchanged a look. Kali and Kori

ducked their heads and popped what remained of their Popsicles into their mouths. Not exactly the eager response Nate had imagined.

"Oh, come on, it'll be fun. The coffeehouse is gonna be great. You'll be able to bring your friends and listen to music and drink sodas and eat muffins...and..." Truth was, Nate wasn't entirely sure himself what exactly went on in a coffeehouse, but he'd imagined it as a good way to occupy his children, give them an insider's view of entrepreneurship and a decent work ethic, provide him with a good excuse to spend lots of time with them, keep their hands busy and allow him to keep an eye on them and their friends. It was one thing for their mother to have granted them the freedom to be "who they are," quite another for their father to be comfortable with their choices. "It's really a cool place," he said, coaxing, hopeful. "And I want your help in choosing paint and decorations and chairs and stuff. I need your help. This is a family project, remember?"

The ensuing silence told him what they thought of his idea. But he pretended not to notice anything out of the ordinary. Come to think of it, this behavior was pretty normal for them. But they'd come around. He was sure of it.

"But I told Ariel—" Cate began.

"Ariel can come with you," Nate offered generously. "This will be a lot more fun than going to the mall. In fact, you can all bring a friend. The more the merrier."

He could see they wanted to argue, probably *would* argue as soon as they figured out the best angle. But they were, as Angie had often remarked, great kids and they didn't say anything. Not now, anyway. And not out loud.

"What time do we have to go?" That was Will asking. As if any time would be too soon.

"Eleven?" Nate suggested. "That gives you plenty of time to…uh, brush your teeth. And change your clothes. If you want. Or ask a friend to join us." He smiled his broadest "Father-Knows-Best" smile. "We're going to have a great time together."

"Great. Just great." Cate flounced toward the door on a sigh, her fringe fluttering with displeasure.

"Just great!" Taking their cue from her, the little girls pushed away from the table and stalked after their sister, carrying their sticky orange Popsicle sticks with them and leaving their sticky orange fingerprints on the table.

It was just the men then, father and son, and Nate looked at Will expectantly.

"Girls are stupid," Will pronounced in his squeaky, changeable voice as he bypassed the freezer and the Popsicles and went straight for the refrigerator and the orange-juice carton. The whole carton, apparently, as he simply opened the spout and took a drink.

Nate would have protested both the observation and the action, except that at thirteen he'd found girls unfathomable, too. He'd also gotten drinks directly from the carton despite being chastised for it repeatedly. Which didn't mean he shouldn't make it an issue. Only now didn't seem to be the prime time to make an issue out of orange juice. "I've been thinking," he said conversationally. "Maybe we could paint the coffeehouse black and call it the Black Sheep? Do you think the girls would go for that?"

Will took another swig from the carton, his somber expression never altering, the traces of the precious little boy he used to be lingered despite the spiky hair and the low-riding denim. "I think we're all pretty much going to hate it no matter what you call it, Dad."

Then he put the orange-juice carton back in the refrigerator, grabbed the milk carton, hooked a bowl with one finger, tucked the cereal box into the crook of his arm and shuffled out of the kitchen.

Nate decided not to think about how his son would manage without a spoon and concentrated instead on his new appreciation for the silence. Taking a sip of his tepid coffee, he went back to wondering what Miranda Danville was having for breakfast.

"What happened to you?" Ainsley asked, her voice sly with innocence.

Miranda didn't even look up. She simply continued leafing through the wedding planner she'd bought on the way to her sister's office. "Did you know," she said in a very conversational tone of voice, "that the best photographers and videographers are booked over a year in advance? Same thing with the better florists and caterers. Hmm." She smoothed her hand across the page, made a note in the right-hand corner. In pencil. "That does make sense, I suppose."

"We're not postponing the wedding," Ainsley said firmly, although just as conversationally. "And you didn't answer my question."

"About the caterer?"

"About what happened to you at Scott's wedding."

"Nothing happened to me at Scott's wedding, except that I went home a bit hungry. We are definitely *not* using that caterer at *your* wedding."

"You know what I meant," Ainsley persisted.

Even as a tiny child, Ainsley had been persistent. Persistently happy. Persistently cute. Persistently persistent. She was the baby of the family, the last born, arriving over an hour after Andrew made his entrance, in no great hurry to dazzle the world with her impulsive presence. Baby, as the whole family sometimes called her, was everyone's favorite. Even Miranda, who had borne the major responsibility for mothering all three of her siblings, had never been able to deny Ainsley much of anything.

Miranda still found it difficult to believe her sister had a real job. Of course, there was some credibility to the argument that matchmaking wasn't a *real* occupation and being a matchmaker's apprentice wasn't a *real* career option. IF Enterprises didn't front for an Internet service that put two people, who'd signed up to be matched with someone…anyone—in touch with each other. IF Enterprises didn't advertise, didn't videotape prospective singles and didn't have a standard fill-in-the-blank questionnaire and application. Ilsa Fairchild, the founder and main matchmaker, was very careful about the clients she agreed to help. Her service was sophisticated, selective and involved in-depth research into each individual's background, likes and dislikes, and romantic history. Research alone sometimes took months, but when Ilsa introduced a client to the possibilities of a romantic relationship, she knew what she was doing.

She had an unheralded record of success, despite the fact that her name was merely a reverent whisper in the ears of New England society. Parents or grandparents with independent-minded children came to Ilsa in private in the hope she could and would agree to arrange an *introduction of possibilities* for their offspring. Bachelors and debutantes, widowers and divorcées, came to her for advice and assistance in matters of the heart. IF Enterprises was the *crème de la crème* of matchmaking services and Miranda was still amazed that Ainsley had convinced Ilsa to take her on as an apprentice. And, despite having a little trouble with the discretion requirement, Ainsley seemed to be thriving in this fairy godmother kind of career.

Which was all the more reason for Miranda to keep her own counsel about Saturday night's encounter with Nate Shepard.

So she merely poised her pen over the planner and looked at her sister over their narrow metal frame. "We have to make some decisions about *your* wedding, Ainsley. Let's not get sidetracked by something you imagine happened to me at Scott's wedding."

"I saw you, Randa, so *tell*."

"There is nothing to tell," Miranda repeated because it was true. And because she wanted it to be true. "Nothing happened."

Ainsley had a magnetic smile...lots of teeth, lots of gum, lots of sparkle...and she flashed it now, her blue eyes, so like their mother's, so like Miranda's own, shining and steady. "You are such a liar, and despite the fact you've been repeating for two whole days that *nothing* happened, I saw you dancing with him and I know *something* was going on.''

Miranda made another note in the margin of the planner. Just a squiggle, nothing she'd ever be able to make sense of later. But it was in pencil and could easily be erased. ''You're imagining things again, Ainsley, and frankly, I don't have all day to spend nailing down some of these details.''

''I'll nail down all the details you want as soon as you've answered my question. You know how curious I am. You know I can't stand not knowing. You know I won't be satisfied until you've told me the whole story.'' She thrummed her fingers on her desktop…as patiently as she ever did anything. ''I *am* your sister. You know you can trust me with the details.''

Miranda laughed, because Ainsley was not known for her discretion. Or her attention to detail. ''Does Ivan know what a provoking child you can be?''

''Ivan knows I'm not a child,'' Ainsley said. ''Someday I hope you'll figure that out, too. And you still didn't answer my question.''

Miranda wasn't altogether comfortable with her baby sister lately. Ainsley had always looked up to her, depended on her, and although Miranda had been anticipating the time when none of her siblings turned to her to solve their problems, now that the time had come, she was finding it a trifle unsettling.

She closed the wedding planner with a sigh. "What exactly do you want to know?" she asked. "And I know you, Ainsley. You've been very busy the last two days, ferreting out all kinds of information about Nate, so let's cut to the chase, all right?"

Ainsley's smile swagged like the Cheshire cat's. "I want to know what you thought about him. I mean, he's handsome. Not like his brother, of course, who is matinee idol/Roman God/too-perfect-to-be-real handsome, but I thought your fella was…well, distinguished-looking. Very attractive in a…distinguished sort of way."

"Yes," Miranda said, wondering if she would have to actually say anything else or if Ainsley would do all the talking.

"His wife died, you know."

"Yes."

"He's twelve years older than Nicky."

Miranda merely arched an eyebrow at that. No point in acknowledging the obvious.

"I think older men are underrated."

"That could be true."

Ainsley's forehead furrowed with curiosity. "So?"

"So?"

"You know what I'm getting at, Miranda."

Oddly enough, she did. "He didn't ask me out," she said, answering the question that hadn't—exactly—been asked. "And if he had, I would have said no. Now, does *that* satisfy you?"

Ainsley frowned, offended. "No. He's very nice, very available, and he liked you. You liked him, too. Don't deny it. Remember, I saw you dancing with him."

"For about half a second," Miranda said in her own defense.

"Then where did you go?"

"Inside the house. He had a stain on his shirt. I suggested he put club soda on it. He said thank-you. I said you're welcome. That's all—*all*—that happened." Except for some errant feelings of attraction. Except for a few sideways glances. Except for a certain alluring knowledge that under other circumstances, *nothing* might have developed into *something*.

"But—"

"He has four children, Ainsley. Two…count them…*two* sets of twins. I'm not interested in raising someone else's children, so don't even think about trying to make this into one of your matches. Remember what happened when you tried to make a match for me with Ivan. It was a disaster."

"No, it wasn't," she protested. "I didn't plan for it to turn out the way it did with Ivan falling in love with me instead of you, but still, even you'll admit that everything worked out for the best. This could turn out nicely, too.''

Miranda admired her sister's optimism, the pure belief in happily-ever-after, which she expressed with such genuine feeling. There had been times in Miranda's own life when she had believed love was the elixir that would make every practical issue moot. When she was still in high school, she'd been seriously in love with Nicky Shepard...until she realized he was seriously in love with himself. In college, she'd dated a number of young men, but nothing had come from the relationships, which was fine with her. She had her hands full trying to guide Andrew and Ainsley through the shoals of their teenage years. Her last serious relationship had been a couple of years ago, with a man she'd convinced herself was her Prince Charming. But when he moved West to pursue a career opportunity, she realized she didn't love him enough to go with him, to choose him over her family. Their engagement had ended painfully, but with no long-term regrets. Since then, she'd come to believe she was too practical for romance, too organized to be swept off her feet. And she did not, under any circumstances, want Ainsley practicing any matchmaking voodoo on her. ''Four children,'' she repeated. ''Two sets of twins. I've raised one family already. I don't want to raise another.''

"But—"

"I've told you what you wanted to know," Miranda continued, ignoring the protest. "Now, let's make some decisions about your wedding." Choosing one of several magazines she'd brought with her, Miranda found the paper-clipped page she was after and held it up for Ainsley to see. "What do you think of having the florist do a floral bower across the sanctuary?"

Ainsley made a face.

"All right." Miranda flipped to the next paper-clipped page. "What about an arbor going up the aisle?"

"Maybe Ivan and I will just elope."

"Don't be silly," Miranda said. "I have lots of other possibilities."

Which she did. All of them for the wedding. None of them for her own future. But that was the way it had always been. She was the caretaker, the mother substitute, the one who made the sacrifices so everyone else could have what they wanted. And right now, Ainsley wanted a wedding, so Miranda was going to make sure it was the most beautiful wedding any Danville had ever had.

And to that end, she proceeded to show the bride-to-be all the floral options she had gathered together, one by one, as possibilities.

IN HER BEDROOM, Cate looked from Kali to Kori to Will. "We have to do something about Dad before he ruins the whole summer."

The girls bobbed their heads in agreement. "I *hate* coffee," Kali announced with feeling.

"I hate the coffeehouse." Will put the problem into perspective.

"I hate coffee *and* the coffeehouse," Kori said, always ready to concur with the majority opinion.

Will sprawled on the floor, his elbows cocked at awkward angles, his hands hooked behind his head, taking up space by virtue of being mainly long and skinny, with long and skinny legs and arms to match. "If I have to go to that stupid old building and talk about Dad's stupid idea for a coffeehouse one more time, I'm going to puke."

"Coffee makes me puke." Kori nodded adamantly, happily repeating words in Cate's room she wasn't certain she was allowed to say in her own. "We should call it a puke house instead of a coffeehouse."

"He's ruining our first summer in Newport." Cate didn't quite know how to stop him, but she knew they had to think of something. "So..." She put the question to the others, "What are we going to do?"

The four of them had been having family meetings for three years, ever since their mother found out she might not get better. Cate hadn't liked the idea then, but she'd gone along because she understood her mom had wanted them to learn to depend on each other, to deal with certain problems as a team. Of course, Mom had meant for the family meetings to include Dad. But Cate and Will had decided there wasn't much point in having the kind of family meeting where one person's vote vetoed the other four, so they'd decided to have family meetings on their own, in addition to the ones they had with Dad. That way, they could work out a strategy to bring him around to their way of thinking before a vote was called. It didn't always work— they were running about fifty-fifty since the move back to Newport—but at least Mom would be proud to know the four of them were learning to work together. At least, that's the way Cate preferred to look at it.

"We definitely have to do something." Will's voice squeaked and he cleared his throat. "Fast."

"Definitely," Cate agreed. "He expects us to clean and paint that nasty building. It may be like 'family time' in his mind, but I think it's like plain old torture."

"It's plain old torture," Kori repeated.

"Family time is supposed to be fun," Kali added.

"So how are we going to distract him?" Cate wished, more than ever, that her mother was still alive. Distracting Dad was one thing she'd been great at doing.

"We could send him on a trip," Kali suggested. "To...to somewhere else. He used to go on trips all the time."

"For the air force," Will said. "He went on trips because the air force sent him on trips."

Kori sighed dramatically. "He's not in the air force anymore."

"We could get him another job," Kali said brightly. "And they could send him on a trip."

Will continued to stare at the ceiling, as if he'd find the answer to their dilemma somewhere up there. "He's not going to get another job in time to save this summer. Whatever the distraction is going to be, it's got to happen soon or the four of us will spend the rest of our school break painting his stupid coffeehouse."

"Stupid coffeehouse," Kori repeated sadly.

"It's got to be someone," Cate said, coming up with an idea. She wasn't sure she liked the idea, but then she didn't like the prospect of cleaning and painting that skanky old building, either. "We've got to find *someone* to distract him, not something."

Will sat up. "Brilliant," he said. "Awesomely brilliant."

Kali and Kori exchanged puzzled looks.

Cate nodded. It was the only possible solution.

"But how are we going to go about finding him a *date?*" Ugh. She didn't like the idea of that either. But this was an emergency. "He'd kill us if we got him a blind date."

"He'll probably kill us if we just tell him he needs to go on a date." Will hugged his knees, thinking hard. "What about the Internet? We might find someone there."

Cate shook her head. "We'd be grounded for the rest of the summer the minute he found out we know how to bypass the computer's parental controls. It's got to be a dating service. A place with real people who can match him up with someone without him knowing about it."

"No one can do that, Cate. Sooner or later, he's going to have to know he has a date."

Sometimes, she wished Will wasn't always so literal. "I heard Grandmother and Maggie talking about a matchmaker. We could ask Grandmother about that."

Kori's eyes widened with excitement. "Let's ask Maggie instead," she suggested. "Maggie will tell us anything…and she'll never in a million years tell Dad we asked."

"Good thinking, Kori." Cate smiled, not exactly comfortable with the idea of her dad dating anyone, but desperate to get out of working on his "family project." "We'll ask Maggie."

Kali giggled. "Maggie will tell us all we need to know."

Kori giggled, too. "This family meeting is adjourned," she said.

Chapter Three

Ainsley held up the fabric swatches, fanning them out in a rainbow, wondering what would happen if she said she wanted one of the bridesmaids in each color. Not that she particularly wanted a rainbow of attendants. Especially not *this* rainbow. But so far her primary enjoyment in this plethora of wedding plans had been imagining what her sister would have to say about various improbable, impractical scenarios.

Miranda, what do you think about serving pie instead of wedding cake? Ivan really likes rhubarb pie and…

Miranda, what about decorating with butterflies instead of flowers? Yes, real butterflies. I saw this magazine article…

Miranda, what if we used a lot of different colors? It would be fun to mix and match the bridesmaids' dresses with the guys' cummerbunds, don't you think?

Ainsley didn't actually mention any of her irreverent ideas to Miranda, but she and Ivan had thoroughly enjoyed imagining what the reaction might have been if she had. She felt a little guilty about laughing, when her sister was going to so much trouble to make everything perfect. And it would be perfect. No doubt about that. Not one of these fabric swatches was anything less than beautiful. Silks, satins, blends. Not a dud to be found among her options. Each fabric was the best in quality, the richest of colors. Regardless of which one she opted for, Ainsley knew Miranda would match everything else in the wedding, from flowers to frippery, down to the smallest nuance of color. The whole affair would be a masterpiece of color coordination, a symphony of shading.

And all Ainsley had to do was choose one color, one single fabric swatch.

I like the Mojave Blue, Miranda had said. *But it's your wedding.*

My wedding, Ainsley thought, distracted by the delicious thought of Ivan. The feeling snuck up on her, out of nowhere, and she hugged it to her heart a dozen times a day. She was going to marry the most wonderful man in the world and, for all she cared, the bridesmaids could wear red feather boas and silver tap shoes.

"You're doing it again." Lucinda, IF Enterprise's wild-child receptionist and secretary, walked into Ainsley's office, message slips fluttering in one hand, a large iced cola cooling in the other. "That dreamy, lost-in-lust smile. Why don't you marry the man and save me the trouble of having to pull you back to boring reality a dozen times a day?"

"Exactly my plan," Ainsley said. "All I have to do is choose the right color." She held out the swatches. "Pick one."

Lucinda gave a little shrug, indicating that her hands were full. "Go with the blue," she advised. "Miranda will look stunning in that color and since it's her wedding…oh, whoops. It's *not* her wedding, is it? Well, since it's *your* wedding, let me give you another word of advice. Choose the color she likes and save yourself the time it'll take for her to change your mind." The message slips drifted down onto Ainsley's desk. "There, see how simple that was?"

"She likes the blue."

Lucinda's eyes widened in patently dramatic surprise. "Sometimes I think I must be clairvoyant."

"Either that or you eavesdrop at the doors."

"That, too." Luci sat on the corner of the desk and sipped her soda.

Ainsley gathered up the message slips, still excited at having her own office and actually getting calls. Not that she got that many, but just seeing her name on the slip was enthralling. She loved the moment of discovery, the thrill of finding out who had called while she was out or otherwise occupied. There had been a time when none of the messages that came in were for her, the matchmaker's apprentice. But lately she was receiving more calls. She even had one client who had sought her out specifically and hadn't been a referral from Ilsa Fairchild. Ilsa Braddock. Ilsa was married now and spending less time providing matchmaking services. Which could be the real reason Ainsley was getting more calls. But she didn't care.

She loved everything about her career. She even loved doing the mountain of research that Ilsa insisted was the foundation for finding the possibilities. There were still moments when she couldn't believe Ilsa had given her this opportunity, couldn't believe such a wise, wonderful woman had seen the potential in her—Ainsley Danville!—and taken her on as an apprentice. It was a dream come true. The work wasn't easy, but Ainsley knew she couldn't have found a more rewarding career field. Even if there were still members of her own family who didn't take her job too seriously. Or believe it could last.

But she didn't mind. She loved her job. Ivan

loved her and was happy that she found her work as satisfying as he found his. And that, really, was all that mattered. That and the progress she was making toward her goal of being a full-fledged matchmaker and not just an apprentice.

She leafed through the slips—four calls. Three of them from Miranda. "Listen to this, Luci," she said, and read one aloud. "'Call church. Make appointment for prenuptial counseling. Ditto caterer.' Does that mean I have to be counseled by the caterer before I can order the cake?"

"Couldn't say," Lucinda replied. "I didn't go the wedding route. Come to think of it, I'm not married. That must be why I'm the calm, down-to-earth woman you see before you. Or wait...it *could* be that I'm still sane because Miranda isn't planning a wedding for me."

Ainsley sighed and exchanged the pink message slips for the Mojave Blue sample swatch. "It's going to be a lovely wedding. You know it will."

"Yes, and you get to wear The Dress."

"*And* marry Ivan."

"And marry Ivan," Lucinda repeated with a grin. "So what are you waiting for? Pick up that phone and set up your prenuptial cake-counseling appointment."

But the phone buzzed suddenly with the sharp

tones that meant Ilsa was calling via the intercom. Ainsley punched a button to answer. "Yes, Ilsa?"

"Could you come into my office, please? I'd like you to sit in on a, uh, consultation."

"I'll be right there."

"Who's in with Ilsa?" she asked Luci, grabbing up her notepad and pen. "Male or female?"

Luci scooted off the desk. "One male, three females."

"Four? That's odd."

"Wait until you see them."

"Why? Are they really old or something?"

"They're really something."

"That's all you're going to tell me?" Ainsley paused at the door and let Lucinda precede her into the hallway. "Once in a while, it wouldn't hurt you to be a little like my sister and tell me more than I really want to know."

"I think they're the potential client's kids," Luci volunteered, although still ridiculously stingy with information. "But I wouldn't swear to it."

Ainsley thanked the receptionist with a roll of her eyes. A potential client's children. That could be interesting. Or not. It didn't often happen that a family member came in to request help in making a match for a parent or child, sister or cousin, but it did happen. The Braddock matches, for instance, had all come about because Archer Braddock had asked Ilsa to find love matches for his three grand-sons. And that had turned out beautifully for all. Ainsley had had somewhat less success playing matchmaker for her cousin, Scott, but that had worked out for the best, too, in the end.

Which only meant that matches resulting from family intervention weren't necessarily a bad thing. In some instances, Ainsley thought they were very nearly essential. Why, she would put together an *introduction of possibilities* for her own sister in a heartbeat if she thought she could get away with it. *That* would give Miranda something besides Ainsley's wedding to obsess over. That would put a damper on some of those sister-to-sister phone calls. That would provide a distraction Miranda badly needed.

Ainsley had asked Miranda to plan this wedding. She'd wanted her sister to handle the details. For one thing, Ainsley wasn't all that interested in the planning part, and for another, she knew Miranda, above all, loved to be needed. For a long time, it had been Miranda who was the caretaker, the one who made certain Matt, Andrew and Ainsley felt secure, were happy, who always put their needs above her own. But they were all grown-ups now, and Ainsley thought it was high time Miranda had an outside interest. Not her landscape-design career, which, of course, she did to perfection. Not the interior designing she referred to as her hobby, but which she did with the same no-holds-barred, list-making attention she gave to everything else. Not the multitude of fund-raising commitments she undertook for the good of the Foundation. No, Miranda needed something that wasn't under her control. A romantic interest. A man who could charm her all the way to her toes, sweep her off her feet and catch her as she fell. Ainsley would love to see that happen to Miranda because she loved her sister and wanted very much for her to find the happily-ever-after she so often denied she wanted. Ainsley would also love to be the matchmaker who facilitated that romance. What a coup that would be.

Ainsley was still smiling at the idea when she walked into Ilsa's office and saw the four little Shepards sitting on the sofa. Well, two of them weren't *little,* exactly. Teenagers or close to it. And she didn't know for certain that they were Nate's children. But she felt it was a good guess, based on a better intuitive feeling. And the fact that two of them were identical twins.

''Hello,'' she said, trying not to show any of her very real surprise. Not so much that the children were here in Ilsa's office. That didn't seem nearly as odd to her as the idea that she'd just been thinking about how to distract Miranda and here, suddenly, might be the opportunity. But she was getting ahead of herself, as she often did. "I'm Ainsley Danville, Mrs. Braddock's assistant."

"I'm Cate Shepherd." The older girl bounced to her feet and stuck out her hand in a way that suggested she was a little nervous. She was young, thirteen at most, Ainsley decided, although she obviously wished to appear much older. Her hair was striking in its oddity—red, blue and a shade closer to banana yellow than blond. Her clothes—low-cut striped capri pants, purple crop top with Who Me? splattered across the front in rhinestones—were designed to make a statement.

What statement, Ainsley wasn't entirely sure, but she shook the girl's hand with solemn formality. "It's nice to meet you, Cate," she said.

Cate made a sweeping gesture with her expressive hands and turned to give her brother a commanding look, then plopped back onto the sofa as if she couldn't think of what else to do.

The boy surged to his feet from a sixty-degree slump, hand outstretched, surprising Ainsley with his height. Andrew had been the same at that age, she recalled. Not so much taller than she had been then, but appearing taller just by virtue of being so lanky and loose-limbed.

"I'm Will," he mumbled.

"Hello, Will," she replied and shook his hand.

He glanced at the two little girls, who remained

seated and somewhat tangled together—one's doggy ear blending in with the other's, two little arms wrapped at the elbow, two legs butted up close as if they had only three legs to share between them. "KaliandKori," he said, running the two names into one. "They're twins." He nodded in Cate's general direction. "And we're twins."

"I'm a twin, too," Ainsley said conversationally, sinking into the remaining chair. "I have an older brother, an older sister, and Andrew, my twin brother."

Kali and Kori exchanged glances, processing this possible kinship.

"They're here about their father." Ilsa leaned forward, the slightest frown at the corners of her mouth. She looked uncertain about what to do with these four youngsters. "We were just discussing him when you came in."

"His name is Nathaniel," one of the little twins said.

"Our mom calls him Nate," the other added. "She died."

"I am so sorry." Ainsley knew this part of the story, but it was suddenly very real to her, reflected as it was in the eyes of these children. "That's an awful thing to have happened. I'm sure you must miss her very much."

The little girls nodded, ready for sympathetic understanding wherever they found it, warming up to Ainsley because she'd offered it. The older two were less accepting, more reticent. "Our dad needs to start dating," the boy said abruptly. "He has too much time on his hands."

Ainsley could hardly sit still, but she kept her composure even as her thoughts went racing off, spinning out a fantasy way ahead of reality. These were Nate Shepard's children. Nate of the near dance with Miranda. Nate of the *nothing happened* dance. Nate of the instant-attraction dance. Nate of the dance that had sparked the *something* Miranda wouldn't admit to.

Sometimes, Ainsley thought, the universe worked in the most mysterious and wondrous ways.

She flipped a page in her notebook, clicked the nib on her pen into position, smiled at the children. "Why did you decide to consult Mrs. Braddock?"

Cate, the apparent spokesperson, spoke up firmly. "We think he, like, needs someone to talk to, someone who'll, like, spend a lot of time with him, someone who'll take his mind off us. Off Mom, I mean."

"Does he want to meet someone?"

"Yes." All four agreed, nodding in unison. "He does. He just doesn't know how."

Ainsley didn't look over at Ilsa, although she wanted to. "So you believe your dad needs a little help…meeting someone."

"That's what we were discussing when you came in." Ilsa angled her chair, so that only Ainsley faced the sofa fully, signaling that she'd be happy for her apprentice to handle this one. "They have some very specific ideas about the kind of woman they'd like their father to meet. I told them you might have some thoughts on the best way to go about this."

Nate. Miranda. Ainsley penned their names side by side onto her legal pad. Perfect. It had *meant to be* written all over it.

"So," Ainsley asked, leaning forward, "do the four of you have someone specific in mind for your dad?"

"Someone fun," the identicals said together, one voice blending into the other. "Someone like our mom," one of them went on to clarify.

Ainsley continued to gaze solemnly at each of the children in turn, letting her gaze linger the longest on Cate's blue-green eyes, acknowledging her as the ringleader of this "let's get Dad a date" effort.

"We don't necessarily want you to find someone he'll want to marry," Cate said firmly. "More like someone to occupy, like, a whole lot of his time. So it'll, you know, like, take his mind off Mom."

Ainsley nodded, trying to fathom the real motive behind this scheme...although she could certainly sympathize. She'd love someone to occupy, like, a whole lot of Miranda's time, too. So it'd, like, take her mind off the wedding. But she didn't say that. What she said was, "No one, of course, can take your mom's place."

Cate nodded. Will nodded. The little ones swung their feet, their attention spans already strained. "But he needs somebody to, uh, help him think about, you know, other stuff," Will said. "And… maybe she could look kind of good."

"Someone who looks…" Ainsley paused to consider. "Someone pretty who can help him think about other stuff." She smiled at Will, beginning to get the gist of this. "You think it would be great if your dad could meet someone pretty who could distract him from whatever's on his mind."

The boy's chin dropped in abrupt agreement with the description and he almost—*almost*—smiled back. "Yeah," he mumbled. "That'd be good."

"Pretty," piped up one of the little ones, latching on to a description she knew. "She has to be pretty."

"Pretty. Distracting." Ainsley made a note on her pad. *Will. Cate. Kali. Kori.* She wrote down their names, then looked at them again with an efficient smile. "Anything else?"

"If she didn't forget things, that could be good." Will's voice squeaked on the last word and he slumped farther down on the sofa cushion.

"Dad's not great with details," Cate explained. "He's kind of forgetful."

"He's old," Kali/Kori said.

"He's forty," confirmed Kori/Kali.

Cate shushed them with a look. "He's forty-four," she informed Ilsa and Ainsley in a tone she probably believed conveyed her abject boredom with adults in general and her father in particular. "Ancient, in other words, but our grandmother, like, thinks he's handsome. Of course, she's his mother and she has to say things like that. Our mother liked him, too, but then she was married to him for, like, forever. But he's not, like, ugly or anything like that."

"Your father's a very attractive man," Ainsley said. "I've seen him."

"You have?" They all looked surprised, as if their father stayed behind closed doors and was never seen by anyone but them. "So you know," Cate said, "that he's kind of a—crash dummy."

Crash dummy? Ainsley wasn't entirely certain what that meant, but she was certain it didn't describe Nate Shepard. Miranda hadn't seemed to think so. But then, Miranda probably didn't know what *crash dummy* meant, either. On the other hand, these were teenagers who judged everyone, especially parents, by their conformity, seeing nothing of interest unless it pertained to themselves.

"So—" Ainsley tapped her pen against her notepad "—you would like us to make a match for your dad. Someone fun, someone distracting, someone who won't mind that he's a little—" she searched for a better word than *crash dummy* "—old-fashioned."

Cate nodded, slowly, obviously not quite hearing the one term she wanted. Ainsley thought about it. "You want your dad to meet someone who can, potentially, occupy a great deal of his time."

"Someone pretty!" One of the identicals again.

"And fun!" said the other.

"Pretty. Fun," Ainsley repeated, smiling to assure the little ones she had their requirements down pat. "So what we need is a woman who is pretty, who's fun, who has a good sense of humor and who can spend a *lot* of time with your dad…but not necessarily want to marry him. At least not right away."

There it was. The shimmer of a smile that started first in Cate's gorgeous eyes and then wrapped down to her lips. Lips painted a garish, incongruous purple-black. "That's right," she confirmed. "Can you find someone like that?"

"It doesn't work quite that way," Ilsa began, but Ainsley impulsively cut her off.

"But sometimes it can," she said, signaling Ilsa with a lift of her eyebrow, letting her know she had an idea of how to handle this rather delicate situation. "I do need to ask—does your dad know you're here? In our office?"

"No."

"No!"

"Noooo."

"No, nuh-uh."

They were definitely in unison on that one.

Will cleared his throat self-consciously. "Our grandmother knows, though. She said it was okay."

Ilsa shot a look at Ainsley, clearly suspicious. "Why didn't she come with you?"

"She's keeping Daddy busy," Kori—or Kali— confided.

"It's a hard job," Kali—or Kori—added with a big sigh.

"We don't want him to know about this," Will said.

Cate sat forward. "We asked Maggie—she's Grandmother's friend—how people like my dad could meet women and she said people like my dad needed all the help they could get. Maggie said you could, like, help. That's why we're here."

Four doggy ears bobbed in agreement. "We want Dad to get help," one of the little girls said.

Probably Maggie had neglected or seen no need to tell these children that IF Enterprises charged a respectful fee for services rendered. But Ainsley wasn't opposed to a little pro bono work. Especially not since the match she had in mind involved her sister. And this would be a perfect match. Ainsley knew it in her heart. Had known it from the second she spied Miranda and Nate together on the dance floor. Of course, she ought to do a little research first—that's the way Ilsa had achieved such a high level of success...by doing meticulous research. But Ainsley knew studying Nate's background, his tastes in books, movies, music, politics, cuisine would only prove her right. And, really, this was something of an emergency. Her wedding was barely three months away. Miranda needed a distraction now. Nate, apparently, was also in need of a distraction sooner rather than later. Waiting could snatch opportunity out of grasp.

Sometimes a matchmaker simply had no choice but to trust her intuition and seize the moment.

Ainsley was, however, fairly certain Ilsa would have one or two legitimate objections, so she rushed on to seal the deal. "You came to the right place," she assured Nate's children. "You just leave this all to me."

Cate stood abruptly and the others popped up as if they were spring-loaded. "Thank you," Cate said. "We'll call you tomorrow to see if you've found someone." Her speech was suddenly formal, grown-up, as she ushered her siblings to the door. "Please don't call the house. Dad has a bad habit of answering the phone.''

''I'll wait for your call.'' Four children, Ainsley thought. Two sets of twins equals four. Miranda would never know what hit her.

''Thank you for coming.'' Ilsa moved forward to see them out. ''Should I call someone to come and pick you up? I'd be happy to ask my chauffeur to drive you home.''

''No, thank you,'' Cate answered politely. ''Maggie's waiting downstairs for us. Dad thinks we're at the mall. Unless you tell him, he won't ever know we've been here to see you.''

''We won't tell him,'' Ainsley assured them brightly, already formulating the explanation she knew Ilsa was going to demand once the door closed behind the Shepard clan. ''At IF Enterprises, we're nothing if not discreet.''

Chapter Four

Painting wasn't actually much fun, Nate decided, assessing the long length of scuzzy white wall still awaiting its new coat of purple. The color already hurt his eyes and he didn't know how he'd let Cate talk him into it. "Get this color, Dad," she'd said, grabbing a sample strip out of the rack in the paint department of Home Depot. "Everybody likes purple. It's snaff, it's pukka, it's fresh."

He didn't understand half the lingo she used these days, but somewhere along the way he'd deciphered *fresh* as slang for *young*—what he and Angie would have called *hip*—and it was that single phrase that had sold him. Opening a coffeehouse along the harbor was something he'd thought of as a great next career. He'd spent years in the military, following rules, interpreting rules, making sure rules were followed by those under his command. It had been a fulfilling career, a good life, but he wanted something simpler now. Something without set-in-stone rules, something he'd have to learn by doing, something that gave him the flexible hours he needed in order to spend time with his kids. Finding this building for sale had seemed like a good omen. He'd imagined working on it with his children, having them help him plan the way it would be set up, deciding the best arrangement for the coffee bar and the stage for the bands, filling the space with laughter and easy conversation even before the doors opened to the public.

He'd imagined that the coffeehouse would be *fresh,* that it would appeal to all age groups, from old to young. But it was becoming apparent the young people he'd most hoped it would appeal to— his own children—weren't very interested. Oh, who was he kidding? They couldn't be less thrilled with the whole concept. Even the little ones, who were usually enthusiastic about all new ideas, good or bad, got wild-eyed with alarm whenever the coffeehouse was mentioned. He figured Cate and Will had told them some horrific story to inspire such panic— and he would get to the bottom of that sooner or later. But the end result was the same—he was here, alone in the big rectangle of old warehouse, painting by himself what he'd envisioned the five of them doing together.

He could have hired a professional crew at the

start and had the whole place painted inside of a week. Two coats, trim work, everything. But no. He'd spent that week doing a song-and-dance routine for his kids, extolling the glories of a paintbrush, rhapsodizing over the good clean smells of fresh paint. He'd been sure he could change their attitude simply by describing the enormous pride of accomplishment that would be theirs, the tremendous thrill they'd feel in having mastered a new skill, the ton of fun they'd have in transforming a tired old place into a shiny new one, the pure satisfaction they'd share in having done it all together.

They'd led him on.

He realized that now. Cate had asked questions, volunteered to help him choose the paint. Will had done research on the Web, checking Consumer Reports for tests on paint durability and something he called pig depth, which Nate could only guess had something to do with pigment. The Kays—as he sometimes called Kali and Kori for short—had listened to him with rapt attention, their duplicate doggy ears bobbing with approval, their eyes bright with excitement right up until the moment he'd mentioned the need to wear old clothes.

Sure enough, when the paint was purchased, the family project ready to begin, his children had—*oops!*—made other plans.

I told you, Dad, like a month ago, I was going to

spend this week with Meghan at the Cape. Her mom said it was okay. You said it was okay. I have to go....

Gee, Dad, I didn't know you meant this week. I've got that basketball camp. Otherwise...

Please, please, please, puh-leeese, Daddy, don't make us paint! We want to help Maggie pack. Please, Daddy....

He should have been rummaging through the Yellow Pages the minute that first excuse hit the airwaves, but no. Pop psychologist that he was, he'd remained cheerful and positive through their domino desertion. He'd smiled as he reminded them they were going to miss out on a great experience, as well as the aforementioned ton of fun. He hadn't lost his cool even once as they tried to shift the blame and make him feel guilty for scheduling a family project when they had other plans. No, sir, through it all, he had calmly practiced the fine art of reverse psychology. It had, after all, always seemed to work well for Angie.

Not so well, apparently, for him.

Even his own mother had advised him to hire a professional painter. Of course, she was full of her own plans, in a hurry to leave for Florida next week and had little inclination for listening to his complaints. *"It's summer, Nathaniel,"* she'd told him in a voice short in tone and patience. *"And they're*

*children. They're not interested in your little paint-
ing project.''*

His little painting project. That was all the coffeehouse was to them. Not the family-bonding experience
he'd planned. Not a direct route to the "Father-
Knows-Best" role he'd hoped to play. Somewhere
Angie was smiling at his delusions of forming a tight
one-for-all, all-for-one unit with his children in one
inventive stroke. She'd told him it wouldn't be easy.

Not that he'd expected instant success—well,
okay, so maybe he had—but he was lonely for the
family life that Angie had wrangled with a firm, con-
sistent aplomb and a fierce, loving, good humor. He
knew the kids were lonely for that, too. And he'd
thought, hoped, the coffeehouse would provide a
way to get some of that family life back.

Instead he was finding out that, like so much of
life without Angie, wrangling a family was a great
deal harder than it looked.

Ditto for painting.

Even with the door propped open and the windows cracked a few inches to catch the breeze off
the harbor, the thick smell of paint hovered like in-
cense in the room and very little air stirred anywhere
in the warehouse. He'd long since discarded his
shirt, and if not for the rhythmic, sing-along beat of
the Bee Gees—the best part of working alone was

that there was no one to make fun of his music se-
lections—he'd probably have hung up his paintbrush, locked the door and gone home. But since no
one was home, either, the Kays having gone shopping with his mother and Maggie, he thought he
might as well keep going and add a few more inches
of purple to the wall before he quit.

It was evident now that the ton of fun wasn't going to materialize, but there was something to be
said for being halfway up a ladder, with a quarter
of purple wall behind him, three-quarters of the day
still ahead and a CD pocket full of the music he'd
loved as a teen. It was, after all, the little things in
life that mattered.

And when he got tired of fresh paint and groovy
music, he'd just pick up the phone and call in the
professionals.

MIRANDA PAUSED to get her bearings, even though
she knew Thames Street like the back of her own
hand. She even glanced, again, at the address she'd
written down on a business card before leaving her
office. As if double-checking her destination would
give weight to her hesitation two doors away.

She was meeting a prospective client. That was
all. Nothing personal. Nothing out of the ordinary.
She met with prospective clients all the time, people
who wanted a landscape design to complement their

home, businessmen and -women who wanted a landscape design to complement their office building.
She talked with people who wanted to change the
look of an existing garden or put a garden where
only lawn had been before. She often contracted to
provide professional maintenance for existing landscaping. She consulted on major projects for the
Danville Foundation and supervised the maintenance of any and all landscaping on the Foundation
grounds. In other words, she was no stranger to
meeting potential customers on their own turf.

So there was no excuse for this anxious excitement percolating in the pit of her stomach like the
follow-up to a sloe gin fizz. This was business.
Strictly business. Tucking the address back into her
bag, she drew in a deep breath, smoothed her lipstick with a press of her lips and walked toward the
building at the end of the block. The one with big
paint cans propping open the double front doors.

Paint cans. What was Nathaniel Shepard doing in
this empty warehouse on Thames Street?

The answer confronted her a moment later when
she stepped inside the cavernous room and was instantly assaulted by the smell of fresh paint, the sight
of more concentrated purple than anyone should
have to see before lunch and the sound of the Bee
Gees at the height of "Stayin' Alive." Nate was
painting. Halfway up a tall ladder, he was trimming

out a windowsill, intent on angling the brush against the wood, singing in a zesty falsetto along with the sound track and completely unaware of her presence.

Which seemed a good thing, considering she was aware enough for both of them.

He wasn't wearing a shirt and his lean muscular back draped in a sinewy taper from his broad shoulders to the waistband of his well-worn jeans. The denim was faded and stretched taut across his narrow hips as he leaned into the windowsill. His biceps flexed with the movement of the brush and a slight sheen of exertion glistened on his skin, casting him, against the purple backdrop, in a fluid bronze.

Who knew a man his age would look so good without a shirt?

Who could have guessed she'd be struck speechless—and slightly breathless—by the simple pleasure of looking at him? Solid, fit, strong and...well, beautifully sexy. She wanted to deny it and wished she could find some other interpretation for this tightening in her body, some logical explanation for the clutch in her stomach. But no matter what she eventually chose to call it, she knew in that moment of awareness exactly what it was. And it went deeper than mere appreciation of a nicely put-together male form. It was more elemental than that. And dangerously, dazzlingly attractive.

Miranda pulled her thoughts up short. She had come here on business. It didn't matter if he was the finest specimen of man ever produced in nature. She wasn't interested. Not in the least. She was here for one reason. He needed help. He'd asked for help. Her help. The phone message, taken down in Ainsley's loopy handwriting, had said Nate wanted to talk about landscaping, that he needed help with shrubs. But that must have been a miscommunication between caller and message taker—Ainsley never paid much attention to detail—because it seemed perfectly obvious to Miranda that Nate required some serious assistance in interior decorating, that he desperately needed help with tints and shades. She couldn't imagine where he was going with this pulsating color theme and she certainly couldn't think of what he might be planning to put with it. She wasn't even sure she wanted to know. But she would do what she could to help him find some way of bringing it all together. Starting with toning down that brilliant, eye-popping purple he was so zealously applying to the walls.

She spent another few idle seconds admiring the view of his bare back before she gathered her wits about her and approached the ladder, self-consciously smoothing the lay of her pale green linen slacks, tugging a little at the hem of her matching linen blazer. "Nate?" she said his name tentatively, then realized he'd never hear her over the music. Pitching her voice to carry over the speakers—which went instantly mute with a lull between sound tracks—just as she screeched, "Hello, Nate!"

He very nearly fell off the ladder.

As he twisted around, paint dripping from his brush, his foot slipped from the rung and he only managed to catch himself by splaying his hand flat against the wall.

The freshly painted purple wall.

"Miranda?" he said, clearly astonished to see her. "What are you doing here?"

She frowned. "We have an appointment."

He frowned, too. "We do?"

"At eleven." Reaching into her purse, she extracted the business card. As if that proved anything. The music came back on and she pitched her voice above it. "You called the house and left a message. With my sister. Ainsley?"

None of that information seemed to ring a bell, because the frown still furrowed his forehead. "I called you," he repeated loudly, obviously trying to remember if, when and why, "and made an appointment?"

"Well, someone called. I just assumed it was you because…" Because that's what Ainsley had written on the card. If that little snip of a matchmaker had manufactured this message out of thin air…"You didn't call?"

He pulled his hand off the wall, swiped it once across his jeans and climbed down the ladder. "Let me turn down the music," he said and headed for the CD player, snatching up his shirt from where it had been draped over the only chair in the large room—a paint-spattered metal folding chair.

"There's paint…" Miranda began the protest too late. He already had the shirt in his hand, was already transferring the paint on his hand to the white fabric. Striding away from her, he stooped down in front of the boom box, giving her a different but equally appealing view of his bronzed bare back, and twirled the knob on the CD player, sending the Bee Gees fading into the background.

But in the ensuing quiet, the rhythms of "More Than A Woman" continued vibrating through Miranda in a fine tension so intimate it bloomed in a seductive heat beneath her skin.

"There," he said, his smile coming around to greet her all over again, even before he rose to his feet and walked back to where she stood, paralyzed by an awareness so intense she couldn't seem to get past it. "Now, maybe, we can get to the bottom of this."

Her first and immediate impulse was to run for the door as if her tail were on fire. But she couldn't get enough breath sucked into her lungs to speak, much less make a run for it. Besides, she didn't run away from her feelings, she wasn't a coward and this was business. Strictly business.

"Hi," he said, pleasure and charm, curiosity and delight all tangled up and blended together in his voice, on his face.

Her heart dropped at his feet like a rock. Okay, so maybe it wasn't *strictly* business.

"Hi," she answered so softly it might have been a prayer. This was embarrassing, she thought, and dropped her gaze from his intriguing brown eyes. It fell first on his bare chest, which seemed much too close for comfort, then dropped to the white shirt still clutched in his hand. "You're getting paint on your shirt."

Glancing down, he seemed surprised to see the shirt in his hand, and then, belatedly, seemed to recall why he'd picked it up. He pulled it on in careless haste, transferring purple blotches of paint in random handprints on the sleeves, on the front panels, the shirttails. Leaving the shirt unbuttoned, he raised a slightly sheepish gaze to hers. "Any chance you have a bottle of club soda in your pocket?"

She smiled. She couldn't help herself. "I'm afraid you're going to need something a little more radical than club soda."

He frowned at the purple splotches. "Turpentine?"

"Scissors," she said. "But, on the bright side, you've just created a great paint rag."

"Good deal. Now all I need is a great painter."

She eyed his hand, the purple paint streaks blending into the crevices in his large palm, fading into tan at the edges. "And maybe some Borax soap to use when you wash your hands."

He looked down, turning his hands from front to back. "Borax, huh? Guess this is one of those occupational hazards."

"You're a painter?"

He laughed. A deep masculine laugh. A laugh that made a woman feel safe, protected...valued. A laugh that soothed doubts and led her to believe he was a man worthy of her trust, a man she wanted to get to know better. "I'd make that claim," he said, glancing ruefully at the purple wall behind him, "but there seems to be a preponderance of evidence to the contrary."

She couldn't help but smile. "I don't think it's your skill that's in question here."

"It's the color, isn't it?"

"When you put some other colors with it, the purple might not seem so...vivid. What sort of look are you going for with this?"

"Fresh," he said promptly. "Snaff. Pukka."

"Oh." Maybe she'd misheard him. "Well, fresh is good."

"No, fresh is young. At least, I think that's what it means. This color was Cate's choice. My daughter. She's thirteen and speaks a foreign language. Something between Sanskrit and sarcasm. I call it Teenglish."

"I remember that phase."

"You do?"

"Sure. When my younger brother and sister—they're twins—were eleven or twelve or maybe even thirteen, they drove me crazy talking in some language they completely made up. Just to annoy me, I think. They, of course, thought it was wildly funny."

"What did your parents do about it? Because I'm lost for ideas."

"My parents?" She sobered some, remembering the responsibility she'd carried, the often overwhelming confusion of being the one left in charge. "They left on another trip, I imagine. They travel a lot for the Danville Foundation. I can't remember them ever being home more than two or three weeks straight."

"Who took care of you and your brothers and sister?"

"I did. Oh, we always had caretakers—a series

of nannies, a succession of live-in help—but mainly I made sure the other three were okay.''

He didn't say anything for a moment, just looked at her, his eyes compassionate, seeing deeper than her words, making her feel he understood what she'd never said aloud. Not even to herself. ''My wife died,'' he said. ''A year ago. Cancer. She was sick for a long time.''

And there it was. A simple statement of fact that somehow linked his experience to hers. A bond. A life-isn't-fair foundation for whatever came after. Miranda didn't plan on anything coming after. Not with this man, who was funny and nice and attractive…and the father of four children. She didn't want to share this basic understanding with him that sometimes life coughed up an impossible choice, made something that was totally unacceptable the thing you had to accept. The absence of her parents was not at all the same as the death of his wife, and yet, somehow she knew he felt their experience was the same. Unacceptable. Unfair. But the thing they had accepted, just the same.

His smile was sudden, leaving the moment intact between them, but shifting the mood like sunlight. ''You know, I'm thinking the one thing that's missing in this room—besides a professional painter or two, of course—is an interior designer. Or a miracle worker.''

"That could be why I'm here."

His eyebrow quirked upward. "You can work miracles?"

"That depends."

"On...?"

"On what you're planning to do with this space."

"A coffeehouse," he answered readily. "Music, cozy nooks, good coffee. Teas. Cocoa. Maybe a few bakery items. But that's pretty much the extent of my creative process."

Nodding, she scanned the rectangle of room, imagining deep, overstuffed couches, chairs and hassocks, pillows, lighted glass blocks forming a coffeeservice island in place of the utilitarian workstation now occupying the center of the room like a putty-colored plywood lump. "A coffeehouse is a great idea. I like it."

"You do?"

She smiled at his surprise. "Yes. Seems like a great niche market to me."

"Well then," he said, a slow grin tucking in at the corners of his mouth, "I guess you'd better get started with those miracles you came here to work."

"I came here because I was under the mistaken idea that we had an appointment."

"Oh, that's right. The mysterious appointment."

She was going to kill Ainsley if this turned out to be one of those ridiculous *introduction of possibil-*

ities she was always talking about. "Not so mysterious, really," she replied. "I think my sister has some tall explaining to do."

He rubbed his chin, leaving flakes of purple paint behind. "I'm inclined to think the explanation is more likely to come from my house. What did the message say?"

"That you were looking for a landscape designer. That you could use some help with shrubs. That I should meet you here at eleven o'clock. Today."

"Shrubs, huh?" He considered the matter. "I'm inclined to absolve your sister from blame, Miranda. I have a feeling this has something to do with my mother. She's preparing to flee the state for a warm winter in Florida and has been lining up all sorts of household projects she wants me to supervise while she's gone. She may have even said something to me about getting a landscape designer. Is that what you do?"

"Yes. Mostly for properties involved with the Danville Foundation, but I take private clients, too."

"And the miracles?"

"I dabble a little in interior design," she admitted. "I did most of the interiors at the new Children's Research Center."

"I don't care who made this appointment," he said. "You're heaven-sent. That's my story and I'm sticking to it."

"But your mother would have told you if she'd made an appointment for you."

"Oh, she'll swear she told me. That's the sort of thing my mother does."

"Like kicking you in the instep to make you dance?"

"Yes, exactly like that." His friendly good humor wrapped around her, made her warm. "But she didn't tell me. Knowing I was going to see you isn't something I could forget."

Miranda, who was almost never uncertain about anything, tripped over her own doubts to fall into his smile. She should not be here. Shouldn't have kept this appointment. She'd been suspicious the minute she'd seen his name in Ainsley's pretty cursive. And yet, here she was, already in over her head in a situation she'd never meant to allow herself to get into.

"So…" Miranda fought for perspective as she pulled a notebook from her bag, scavenged a pencil from the depths of her Kate Spade. She needed to concentrate on maintaining a businesslike manner, and to stop getting distracted by the flecks of gold in his eyes, the tiny chip in his right front tooth, and the fact that she'd almost danced with him. "We should talk about what kind of landscape design your mother wants."

"I don't have the foggiest idea and, just so we

understand each other, I'm not wasting any miracles you can do on the lawn at home. I want this coffee-house open by Halloween. Can you help? Will you?''

No was the correct answer. She knew that. But the words that came out of her mouth, straight from her suddenly foolish heart, were, ''Yes. Yes, of course I will.''

Chapter Five

"Don't move," Nate said.

He lifted his hands with the half-formed intention of guiding her to the only seat in the house, but remembered in time that he had paint on his hands. And if he touched her, he'd get paint on her and she'd have to go home and change clothes. And she probably wouldn't come back. And the metal folding chair wasn't anything a woman like Miranda would want to sit on, anyway. So he modified his plan, holding his hands, palms out, in a *stay* gesture as he backed toward the door. "I'll be right back. Ten minutes tops. You can change the CD if you want. Or you can switch it to the radio. Or you can turn it off. You can do anything you want. Just… wait for me. Please." Then, with one last lingering, entreating smile—really, she was quite breathtakingly pretty as she stood looking at him, her forehead furrowed, hesitation written into the slight angling of her body—he reached the door, turned reluctantly around and hurried through it.

Nine and a half minutes later, he was back with a loaf of bread, a jug of wine and a book of verse. Okay, so it was just deli sandwiches, two pop-top cans of soda and a clean shirt. No paint stains. Only a slight tear in the underarm seam where he'd ripped out the price tag. But he didn't think she'd notice that as long as he kept his arm down. He hadn't been in this state of anxious excitement since…he couldn't remember since when. Maybe since the day he'd proposed to Angie. No, not even then, as he'd been certain—or reasonably so—that she wanted to marry him as much as he wanted to marry her.

Not that he wanted to marry Miranda. Wasn't even thinking about marriage. Well, he was thinking about it, since he'd had to stop and clarify in his own mind that he was not thinking about it. But this had nothing to do with that. This was about anticipation, possibilities. This was knowing an attractive woman was waiting for him, that there was a veritable fireworks display of sparks whenever they occupied the same space. This was mystery, magic, the prospect of something he wasn't sure he felt comfortable giving a name.

But it had been some time since he'd felt anything this close to exciting and he resolved to enjoy the hopeful suspense for as long as it lasted. Maybe she

hated plastic-wrapped turkey and Swiss on wheat.
Maybe she loved 7-Up. Maybe she hated that he'd
left her so abruptly. Maybe she'd love that he'd left
to scrub his hands and buy a clean shirt from the
boat supply across the street. Maybe she was still
waiting for him. Maybe she wasn't.

She was.

His heart beat faster as he stepped into the room
and saw her. "You waited," he said.

She spun around—she'd been at the wall opposite
the one he'd been painting—holding out a pencil as
if he'd just caught her writing graffiti on the bath-
room wall. "Oh, you startled me," she said, her
surprise giving way to a slow, reticent pleasure, her
eyes turning azure with a subtle smile. "You
changed your shirt."

He was ridiculously pleased that she'd noticed, a
little smug that he'd known something so small
would please her. "The other one had a stain on it,"
he said. "I couldn't wear it through lunch."

"Lunch?"

"You know…no shoes, no shirt, no service?"

"Oh." She glanced at her watch. "I didn't realize
it was almost noon. You probably have a luncheon
engagement. I can come back another time and talk
to you about this." Her hand fluttered toward the
wall behind her. "I was only sketching out a couple
of ideas. You can paint right over them."

"Why would I do that?" He walked toward her, the sack of sandwiches and soda in the crook of his arm. She took a backward step, bumped the wall, came away from it, dusting the back of her slacks. She'd taken off her jacket, had folded it so it rested on top of her purse on the floor, not touching anything except the purse. She glanced at it now and he could see she was wishing she'd kept it on. Why she wished that, he wasn't entirely sure, because she looked very nice in just the slacks and silky, sleeveless top. And she had to be cooler. But he sensed she was nervous, that he made *her* nervous. Which was not at all the effect he wanted to have. "I was hoping you'd stay and have lunch with me," he said, casually putting the sack down on the plywood workstation. "If you don't like deli sandwiches, I could order a pizza or something."

"You brought sandwiches?"

"Turkey and swiss. It was all Dave had in the refrigerator. It's all he ever brings for lunch. Dave's my friend," he explained, gesturing vaguely toward the door and the world outside it. "He owns the boat supply across the street. He sold me the shirt, gave me the sandwiches and let me use his washroom to clean up. He keeps Borax soap on hand for manly mishaps."

Her gaze drifted to his hands, newly scrubbed,

void of all but a faint tinge of purple. "Dave gave you his lunch?" she asked.

"Well, not exactly. I had to barter for it. I got the sandwiches, he gets free coffee over here for the rest of his life."

"Sounds like you got the worst end of that deal."

"If you stay for lunch, believe me, I'll have gotten the best of the bargain."

Her eyes met his, skittered away, and Nate felt the jolt of awareness rip through him again, saw her hand clench the pencil. This was, he decided, just a little intense for the lunch he had in mind. "We can talk about your ideas for the coffeehouse over Dave's sandwiches, what do you say?"

He began unpacking the sack, taking out a box of laminated cork place mats—a set of four, featuring various sailing scenes, which Dave sold as a tourist item in the boat-supply store. Upending the box, Nate looked for a seam in the shrink-wrap plastic, wondering why everything these days had to be wrapped and sealed with such minute precision, thinking he probably should invest more heavily in the plastic-wrap industry.

"You bought place mats?"

He tried to work his thumbnail under the plastic. "If I'd had ten more minutes, I'd have come back with a table and chairs. But I didn't want to push my luck."

"Luck?"

"Asking you to wait even ten minutes seemed like a gamble."

"I'd have waited thirty," she said. "Probably longer."

His hand lost its hold on the box, but he caught it again before it dropped.

"I don't have another appointment until two," she went on. "And I tend to get caught up in ideas anytime I start a project. I love a challenge, and this—" she let her gaze wander the room "—kicks my creative impulses into overdrive."

Damn, she was pretty. And the impulses she kicked into overdrive in him didn't have much to do with creativity. Well, maybe they did. He fumbled with the box again, losing the nick he'd managed to make in the plastic wrap. "I'm glad you have ideas for the coffeehouse," he replied. "That means you'll stay for lunch."

She seemed to assess him and his statement for a moment, then she walked over to where she'd left her purse and jacket.

Nate was suddenly certain she was going to leave and wondered what he'd said and, more importantly, what he could say now to stop her.

But when she turned around, the purse and jacket remained behind and all she brought with her was a small pair of scissors. Without a word, she snipped the plastic. "There," she said. "You looked like you needed a little help."

He named the *something* then. Called it what he'd known all along that it was...this intoxicating sense of possibility that was the beginning of a relationship. *Romance.* That was what he felt, what he believed she felt, too. The *something* that had the potential to be *something more.* "Thank you," he said, not knowing what heavenly chance had her keeping an appointment he hadn't made. Not caring if his mother wanted shrubs or if her sister had written his name by some bizarre, divine accident. He only cared that she was there. And that she hadn't changed the CD.

"Lunch is served." He spread the place mats across the plywood workstation, pulled the sandwiches and sodas from the sack and offered her one of each. "Tell me your ideas."

WHEN HER CELL PHONE began ringing, deep within the pocket of her purse, Miranda was sketching another design possibility for the coffeehouse onto the wall. "If you put the station here—" she penciled a quick three-sided rectangle "—you'd have the advantage of distance from the stage."

"And if we added another one over here—" he duplicated her sketch, flopping it so his drawing of a rectangle faced hers, and then penciling thick arrows shooting back and forth ''—we could have dueling cappuccino contests.''

She laughed as she walked toward her purse to retrieve the phone. Nate was such a curious mix of seriousness and fun. He gave equal weight to her every suggestion, seemed to find merit in them all, discussed the pros and cons with grave consideration, and then out of the blue, he'd make some off-the-wall remark that surprised her into a laugh. She dug out the phone, still burring its demand for attention, and glanced idly at her watch. *Two-thirty!* Her heart gave a thump of alarm. How could it possibly be two-thirty?

''This is Miranda,'' she said into the palm-size phone.

''And this is Ainsley,'' came the perky voice from the other end. ''You're late.''

Miranda was never late. She prided herself on being both punctual and organized. She didn't forget things, didn't let other things distract her. Not until today. Not until Nate.

''I'm sorry.'' Honesty was the best policy here, because a lie wouldn't have stood a chance. One way or another, she was going to endure a good deal of teasing from her sister. ''I completely forgot. I'll be right there.''

''No, stay where you are. There's no need to rush away from whatever you're doing, because Ivan and

I took care of it. We handled the whole thing and we've already finished with Captain Video, anyway. But we're dying to know what happened to you.''

Miranda closed her eyes, not wanting to admit what—or more accurately, who—had distracted her. ''An unexpected delay,'' she answered crisply, as if it had been unavoidable. ''Did you take plenty of notes? We'll want to compare product and pricing with the other two videographers Andrew recommended.''

''No notes were necessary,'' Ainsley said brightly. ''Ivan and I liked this one, so we hired him. One more item off your list, Randa.''

''We talked about this last night, Baby, and agreed to look at all the options before deciding. Remember?''

''Well, this is one less option we need to consider. Captain Video was very nice. I liked him. Ivan liked him. You'd have liked him if you'd been here. He has a good product and so we hired him. Now, we can all move on to the next item.''

There was a note of decisiveness in Ainsley's animated voice, a hint of new confidence in her tone. Miranda heard it, felt her sister's resolve, and couldn't decide if this new maturity should be credited to Ivan or to the possibility that she was, actually, finally, growing up. Miranda was more than ready for that change to come and felt equal measures of pride and exasperation over what had turned out to be a long, lingering process. As hard as it was at times to believe, her baby sister was about to be married. It was time Ainsley took on the responsibility of making her own decisions and stopped depending on Miranda to take up the slack.

Which only meant that if Ainsley and Ivan were happy with Captain Video, then Miranda would be happy with him, too. "Great," she said brightly. "I'll look forward to hearing all about the videographer tonight at dinner."

"What *kind* of unexpected delay?" Ainsley asked slyly, her voice switching from the tone of fledgling maturity into a little sister's singsong wheedle...*I-know-what-you're-doing.* Honestly, ever since she'd started working as a matchmaker's apprentice, she thought she was too cute for words. Miranda was beginning to think she was too cute to live.

"I'm with a client," Miranda said. "I'll talk to you later." And she snapped the phone case closed.

"You missed your appointment." Nate's expression was the perfect blend of apology at being the cause, curiosity about the missed appointment and a calm, rather jaunty acceptance that sometimes time slipped away and appointments got missed. "I hope it wasn't anything that can't be rescheduled."

"As it turns out, my sister handled it. Captain Video will be the one videotaping her wedding."

She tucked the phone back into her purse and turned toward him. "I was supposed to meet her at his office, but I forgot." The weight of the words—*I forgot*—was foreign on her tongue. She couldn't believe she'd just uttered these words, that they were, unarguably, true. "I can't believe I did that," she said, self-recrimination churning inside her.

"Everyone forgets occasionally, Miranda."

"I don't. I pride myself on never being late and I don't forget appointments. Ever. I just don't do that sort of thing. I'm very organized. I've had to be."

His lips quirked into a smile. "Then it's definitely your turn."

Her turn? To do what? To be distracted by a man—however charming and attractive he might be—to the point that she completely lost track of time? To forget who she was and what she was supposed to be doing? No, thank you. She quickly began gathering her things, unfolding her jacket, trying to slip one arm through the sleeve, surveying the room to see if she'd overlooked any personal item. "I have to go," she said.

He was beside her then, lifting the back of the jacket so she could get into it without a struggle. "When can I see you again?"

Her heart gave a foolish jerk of longing, her stomach took a nosedive. *When can I see you again?*

That sounded personal, provocative. A prelude to something that wasn't strictly business. "Consider this a contribution," she replied, waving vaguely at the dozen or so pencil sketches on the wall. "I didn't spend that much time on it, so feel free to choose the layout you want, with my blessing."

"Oh no you don't." His hands rested lightly on her shoulders, turning her around with an almost ludicrous lack of effort. "I know how that sort of arrangement works. You'll be in here the minute the doors open, expecting free coffee from now until the bells of heaven ring. I'm paying you your going rate."

"You can't afford me." The quip was all air, self-defense in a bubble of throwaway words. Of course he could afford her fees. His family name might not be as old as hers, but his family fortune was nothing to sneeze at either. She knew that. And what's more, he knew that she knew. But she attempted a smile nonetheless, a camouflage for her embarrassing lack of tact. "You've already gotten the best of me, anyway. The best of my ideas, I mean."

"I don't think so," he said simply. "I really need your help in pulling this place together, Miranda."

His hands remained on her arms, a light unobjectionable grip just below her shoulders that interfered, somehow, with her ability to think. She had to make it clear that she couldn't work for him. With him.

Nate was too…distracting. He was the reason she'd forgotten the Captain Video appointment, the indirect cause of this uncharacteristic lapse of memory. She should never have stayed for lunch, but hearing he'd bought a new shirt just to please her was…well, absurdly flattering. And place mats. He'd bought *place mats*. The simple thoughtfulness of that had startled her, thrown her off balance. And then, almost before she'd completely made up her mind to stay, he was asking questions. Questions about her. When she'd developed an interest in design work. How her eye for color worked in landscaping. Which she liked more. What book she was currently reading. What she thought about them both being on the ballot for city council, albeit from different wards. What she'd like to see happen in the State Senate race. Was she a Celtics fan or was baseball her game. Did she really like the Bee Gees or was she only being nice.

There was no getting past it. Nate Shepard had gotten around her defenses, reached a corner of her heart she kept private and off-limits. They'd talked about everything and nothing, laughed over little things, shared a Twinkie one of his daughters had left behind on a previous visit.

A *Twinkie!*

Clearly, Miranda had to get out of here and give herself some breathing room. "I'm glad I could help, Nate. You have a great concept here. But I'm too busy at the moment to take on another client.''

His expression changed, and for a moment he simply looked at her, his steady gaze making her uncomfortably aware of how close he was to her, how close she was to him, how big a lie she'd just told. ''It's too late for that, Miranda.''

''Too late for what, Nate?''

''The brush-off. That is what this is, isn't it?''

She swallowed, sensing a trap, no matter what answer she gave. ''I don't know what you're talking about.''

He frowned, a look that was a little uncertain but still dangerously confident. ''I'll admit I'm out of practice, but I still know when a woman is trying to tell me she's not interested.''

''I didn't say that.'' And she *wished* she hadn't said *that*. ''I mean, I really am busy and…''

''I like you, Miranda.'' He disarmed her again with his simple sincerity. ''I'd really like to see you again. I want to get to know you better. I want to spend time with you.'' His gaze drifted to her lips, returned to her eyes. ''This probably is as much a surprise to you as it is to me, but I'd really like to…kiss you.''

Her heart skipped a long beat. Maybe because she'd stopped breathing. Maybe because he wanted to kiss her. Maybe because she wanted him to. ''I, uh…'' She couldn't seem to find a coherent reply. ''I don't…uh, know…what…you mean…by surprise.''

"Then let me be more explicit." His hands drew her forward, then moved up to cup her chin, to cradle her face in his palms, giving her time to protest or to pull away. But she didn't. She stood there, mesmerized, confused, lost…until his kiss found her.

His lips brooked no resistance, hers offered none, and the kiss was instantly deep, infinitely tender, intensely deliberate. Her eyes fluttered closed as her hands gave in to the longing to slide up to his shoulders, as her body leaned into his. He pressed his lips into the curve of hers, made no secret of the pleasure he found there, and asked only that she return the favor. There was no pretense in his kiss…it was seduction, intention and truth, all layered into a few, sweet, tantalizing moments. She could call the attraction whatever she wanted after this, but they would both know it was something more.

The warmth of his hands on her face, the steady tenderness of his palms against her skin offered strength and encouragement, support and expectation. He didn't demand her participation as much as he simply took it for granted…and that, she discovered, was incredibly seductive. Miranda was not a complete stranger to passionate kisses and the sure embrace of a man, but she felt unprepared for this tender assault on her senses. This practical magic. She'd been kissed before, but not, she realized now, by a man who truly understood how it should be done. Not with the patience Nate displayed. Not with the sweet wisdom he inherently conveyed that pleasure was, in itself, enough reason for a kiss to be.

Nate had experience in pleasing a woman, enough practice to be efficient, enough maturity to be good. Better than good. Like it or not, he had just raised the standard for a first kiss. Or any subsequent kiss, for that matter, and at the moment, all she could do was enjoy the knowledge that she was in very capable hands.

When he pulled back, his eyes appeared darker, the golden flecks burned to a dusky amber. Or maybe it was her own passion-blurred vision that had him slightly out of focus, like a filtered photograph, all soft edges and romantic undertones, with only determination clear and unmistakable at its center. ''Before you walked in here this morning, I could have gone either way on this, Miranda. But I'm not willing to do that now. There's something happening here between us, something I mean to explore.''

Miranda willed her eyebrows to rise, her eyes to widen, as if she was surprised…shocked…as if he had noticed something she had failed to detect. "I'm not looking for a relationship."

His smile mocked her unworthy attempt at denial. "I don't want to frighten you. Hell, I'm scared enough for both of us. But the last few years have taught me some important lessons, one of them being that while we have all the time in the world to explore and enjoy whatever this is that's happening between us, we haven't a moment to waste in denying that it exists." His thumb stroked softly along her cheek, and her lips parted with expectation, with sudden, swift desire, confirming what he knew and what she was still reluctant to admit. "I intend to spend as much time with you as possible, Miranda, whether we're discussing gardens or paint color or the possibility of life on Mars. I want to know you…and you can take that as a compliment or as a challenge."

She swallowed hard, summoned her considerable pride and pulled away. "I should go," she said.

"Probably a good idea," came his answer. "Otherwise, I may put you to painting."

She picked up her purse from the floor, dusted the bottom with a swipe of her hand and recovered a remnant of cool professionalism. "I'll get you the name and number of a good contractor."

"Great. I'll look forward to hearing from you."

His wry, warm smile altered her plan to walk out the door unscathed.

And she had to be content with simply walking out.

NATE WATCHED HER GO, the taste of her still on his lips, the scent of her still lingering sweetly in the folds of his new shirt. He'd just kissed Miranda Danville. And Miranda Danville had just kissed him back. Amazing.

He rubbed his hand across the placket of his shirt and fought the impulse to go to the doorway and watch her walk down the street until she was out of sight. But he didn't. He simply stood there, remembering the kiss, wondering if he should feel something other than bemused excitement. He didn't know the procedure for opening his heart to love a second time, wasn't sure if any rules existed. He'd been married nearly twenty years, had been a widower for one. There wasn't a question in his mind that he would always love Angie, always miss her. And yet, there was no question in his heart that the kiss he'd just shared with Miranda was the sweetest he'd ever known, and that he wanted to repeat it at the first opportunity.

He pondered how those two facts could exist side by side and both be equally true. He wondered if he had the courage to risk loving again, with its accompanying possibility of loss.

But he understood that the attraction, the *spark*, he felt for Miranda was worth pursuing.

And that's what he intended to do.

Chapter Six

Miranda tucked her clipboard in the crook of her arm and reached forward to ring the doorbell. Beyond the door, she heard the deep tonal chimes and straightened, adjusted the strap of her purse, settled the clipboard more securely and told herself—for the millionth time—that she was *not* nervous. Why *would* she be nervous? She had come here on business. She made this type of call, did this same sort of preliminary evaluation every time she took on a new client. This was nothing new. Yes, this was Nate's home. Yes, he had kissed her. But that was no reason to treat this any differently than she would any other job.

She was inclined to blame her sister for this edgy feeling. Ainsley, with her crafty smiles, her artful asides, her sly glances carrying the underlying message that, as a matchmaker, she knew *something* had happened and that she wouldn't rest until she discovered what. It had been three days since Miranda's meeting with Nate at the coffeehouse. Three days in which the matchmaker's apprentice had gone to great lengths to ferret out the details of what had happened. Three days in which she had come up with dozens of seemingly offhand questions designed to inspire a slip of the tongue, a careless admission. But Miranda had been ready for her, had been cool, calm and casually nonchalant about the nature of the meeting. Not once had Ainsley come close to getting what she was after.

Because, of course, there was nothing for her to get.

Miranda had thought a great deal—rather more, actually, than she'd wanted to—about Nate's kiss and his startling declaration. She'd first decided to ignore the whole thing, send him the name of a painting contractor, refer him to another landscaper, and avoid him and the unpleasantness of having to explain why she wasn't interested in pursuing the attraction. Or whatever it was. But upon reflection, she'd decided that looked too much as if she was afraid to pursue it. Which she wasn't. But she wasn't interested in a ready-made family, either. If Nate's children were older, well, perhaps she could have seen more possibilities in letting the attraction run its course. But his children were young. And motherless. She didn't want to raise another woman's children. She didn't. Been there, done that. And even if she was thinking too far ahead—after all, it had only been one kiss—there was no point in allowing a relationship to form when she knew, at some point, she'd have to end it. Or change her mind.

Still, she'd expected a rush. A phone call, at least. Maybe the courtship ritual of flowers first, followed by an invitation to dinner. Nate seemed like an old-fashioned guy, someone who would appreciate the value of a little romancing. He did not seem like the sort of man who would first tell a woman he wanted to spend as much time with her as possible and then not follow up on it with action. But he didn't call. No flowers arrived. No invitation was delivered. No romancing ensued.

Which could only mean he'd either come to his senses or was giving her plenty of time to think about what he'd said and anticipate his next move. The latter was, in her opinion, a tactical error on his part, because it gave her plenty of time to rehearse a brief, no-nonsense refusal of any overture he might make. She even came up with a few firm, slightly apologetic words of closure, which she would offer if he pressed her.

All of which merely firmed her resolve to stand her ground. Nate had issued a challenge and she had no intention of letting it go unanswered. She'd been kissed before and it had never stopped her, never sent her running for cover. Nate lived in Newport. They moved in the same social circles. He was running for, and would probably win, a seat on the city council. Avoiding him would be impossible.

So she'd taken a couple of days to plan her strategy, then she'd phoned Charleigh Shepard and arranged this two-thirty appointment. The fact that she knew, via a chatty conversation with the painting contractor, that Nate wasn't at home, that he was, in fact, at the coffeehouse meeting with the contractor even as she rang his doorbell, was simply good planning on her part.

As she stretched her hand toward the doorbell a second time, there was a sudden scrambling noise on the other side of the big, wooden doors, the sound of scuffling, and then the click of the latch as it opened. A moment later, two pairs of wide brown eyes were staring at her from inside the foyer, two identical faces looked back at her, two moppets with identical freckled noses, identical pink-checked rompers and beribboned doggy ears regarded her with suspicion. "If you're a stranger," one of the moppets said, "you'd better leave because we can't talk to you."

"Are you a stranger?" the other moppet inquired.

"Yes and no," Miranda answered. "If you'll find

your grandmother, she can introduce us and then I won't be a stranger anymore.''

This elicited consideration in the form of duplicate stares, followed by the abrupt slamming of the door. She heard the animated murmur of their voices on the other side, probably arguing over who should go for reinforcements and who should stay to guard the door. Miranda hadn't raised a set of twins without learning something about the way they thought, and she suspected they both wanted to be the one left to defend the door. She wasn't at all surprised when she heard them screeching for their grandmother at the top of their lungs.

A few minutes later, Charleigh Shepard opened the door with an apology for her granddaughters' heathen display. The twins, introduced as Kali and Kori, seemed subdued by their grandmother's gentle scolding but Miranda suspected they were far from being swayed by it. They continued to keep a close eye on her as she and their grandmother exchanged greetings and talked about the garden project.

''I know this isn't the right time of year to be landscaping,'' Mrs. Shepard said as she led the way down the front steps, with Miranda beside her, the twins whispering fiercely to each other behind them, ''but I do hope you'll be able to come up with some ideas that will get us on the right track for spring.''

''I'm sure I can, Mrs. Shepard. There are actually

quite a number of options for fall and winter gardens, too.''

''Wonderful.'' Mrs. Shepard walked around to the east side of the house, where a huge sycamore showed the first tinge of autumn color, a hint of flaming red that was echoed in other trees across the acreage. Close to the house, however, the shrubs and plants looked overgrown and untended, listless and forgotten. There was even one section, beside a cold, gray concrete bench, where the only shrubbery was a bramble of dead and dying bushes. In a regretful gesture, Mrs. Shepard swept a hand outward to encompass the sad state of her gardens. ''I'm afraid I've neglected them terribly the past couple of years.'' Her long, wizened fingers drifted down to touch a leggy rosebush, brushed across the fronds of a scruffy fern. ''I used to tend it all myself and should have hired a gardener to take over when I lost interest, but somehow I never did. Having a lovely garden didn't seem very important once my daughter-in-law became ill.''

Miranda listened respectfully as she made a couple of notes on her clipboard pad and began to sketch a rough drawing of the garden perimeters and its layout onto the paper.

''You know about Angie, I imagine,'' Charleigh continued. ''Newport is still, occasionally, a small town in many ways. At any rate, with Nate and the children living here now, I think it's time to update the grounds. We're leaving for Florida on Sunday, planning to stay the winter there, and this way I can look forward to seeing it completed when I return next spring.'' She laughed softly. ''You can see the devious nature of my thinking, Miranda. This way, I'll experience none of the inconvenience but all of the pleasure.''

We're leaving. Plural. Miranda's heart caught on a tiny flap of disappointment. Which was ridiculous as, if Nate left, she wouldn't have to worry that he would be home and causing a problem for her. ''So you're all going to Florida,'' she said, trying to make it sound as if she thought that a grand idea. ''How nice.''

''Oh, no,'' Mrs. Shepard told her quickly. ''Only Maggie and I are heading for sunnier climes. Maggie is my dear friend and has worked for me so long I can't imagine going anywhere without her. Which does mean, Miranda, that whatever you need, Nate will be happy to get for you. He may have some ideas he'd like incorporated into the gardens. The house, after all, is actually his to do with as he likes. It's been far too large a place for me all these years, anyway. I was merely holding it in trust for a time when one of the boys wanted to make it a home for their own family. As I'm sure you know, Nicky has never had much inclination in that direction.''

"I haven't seen Nick in a long time, but I do remember him as being more...well, more wings than roots."

"You put it very nicely, Miranda. He's a hellion, but I still have hope that one day he'll come to his senses and settle down." They'd reached the back of the house and Mrs. Shepard took the steps up to the terrace. Miranda followed, but the twins hovered at the base, discussing some unknown topic behind raised hands.

"If it's all right, I'd like to spend a little time wandering around, thinking about the best way to rejuvenate your garden." Miranda clipped the Pentel to the top of the clipboard, smiled at Mrs. Shepard, thinking how much she liked the woman, how fortunate Nate and Nick had been to have such a mother. "I won't be too long."

"Take all the time you want." Mrs. Shepard gave permission with a wave of her hand. "And feel free to come again anytime. You don't even need to call ahead unless you want to talk to Nate. He isn't here much during the day...but someone will be here. Maggie and I will be gone after Sunday, but there will be a nanny or some such person to look after the children when their father isn't home. He's spending a lot of time lately at that building he's renovating downtown." She offered Miranda an appreciative smile. "He mentioned that you had been there and that you have some great ideas for his little project.''

''As a matter of fact, I did meet with him briefly.'' Miranda said it as if she had only just recalled the encounter, as if it had no more significance than any other appointment in a busy day. ''In fact, I believe you set up that appointment so I could discuss the landscaping with Nate.''

The older woman's smile turned noncommittal. ''Did I? My memory isn't as dependable as it once was. But I do sincerely thank you for offering those suggestions to Nate. I know he needs the help. I'm very pleased, too, that you've agreed to take on the task of healing my garden. I'm sure you'll do a perfectly wonderful job. Now, go anywhere you want, do whatever you need to do…and don't let the children haunt you. They can be quite persistent at times.''

''They won't bother me, Mrs. Shepard.''

''I hope not. Maggie's gone to the grocer's and I have to leave in a few minutes to run an errand. There seems to be some confusion over the boxes we're shipping to Florida and I can't get it straightened out over the phone. I won't be gone long, and Cate is here to watch the girls. Send them inside to her if they become a problem.''

''I'm sure that won't happen.''

''I hope not. They can occasionally be quite in-

corrigible. Kali? Kori? Best behavior.'' Mrs. Shepard called out the instruction to the girls, who were
clustered like a two-player football huddle at the
foot of the stairs. They looked up at their grandmother, all innocence, then returned immediately to
the huddle when she entered the house. Miranda regarded the twins for a moment, wondering what they
were discussing with such energy, thinking it probably had little if anything to do with her. She flipped
to a fresh page and began making notes even before
she reached the bottom of the steps, where she
walked past Kali and Kori on her way around the
house to the side garden.

Their observation was furtive at first, but quickly
grew bolder. Their whispers got louder, their giggles
more frequent, and they became very noisy shadows, darting behind shrubs, ducking out of sight if
Miranda so much as glanced in their direction. She
figured it was best to let them approach her—or
not—at their own pace, and went about her work,
sketching out the garden and grounds, pretending to
be unaware of their keen surveillance.

Then, without warning, the rules of the game
changed; they were at her heels and the inquisition
had begun.

"What's your name?"

"Where do you live?"

"What are you doing?"

"Why are you writing things down?'
"What are you drawing?"
"What kind of pencil is that?"
"Do you have a little girl?"
"Do you like Popsicles?"
"What's that called?"
"What's a weed?"
"Why do people have gardens?"
"How do you make a garden?"
"Do you have a goldfish?"
"Why do fish float when they die?"
"Do you like pink eye shadow?"
"Why is your hair that color?"

Their curiosity appeared endless, their questions seemed a constant natural spring bubbling up and out of them. Miranda answered each and every inquiry with patient good humor, remembering when Andrew and Ainsley had been quiet only while asleep, remembering her childish frustration at their never-ceasing babble, recalling her ever-present worry that something terrible would happen to them before her parents returned and her sometimes horrible wish that it would. She had been too young for the responsibility she'd assumed, too fearful of disaster not to take it on. No one had ever said she should be the surrogate parent, and to this day, she didn't know if her parents fully realized that's what she became in their absence.

Matt, Andy and Ainsley knew. They'd resented her for it at times, she knew, but mostly they'd allowed her to take charge, depended on her to make the decisions, to bear the burden of responsibility. Matt, being two years older than Miranda herself was, had gone along with her directives when it suited him and did what he wanted when it didn't. But the twins... They had needed her. Sometimes overwhelmingly. Sometimes not so much. It was a miracle, Miranda thought, that the four of them had managed to grow up with their relationships intact, that they not only recalled their odd childhood with affection, but with genuine nostalgia.

She could take credit for that. Her sacrifice had made Danfair a home; her resolve had kept the family from disintegrating. She didn't fault Charles and Linney for their commitment to a great cause. But she didn't feel they deserved great praise for their choices, either. They'd chosen to have children, then relegated them to the background of their lives, providing for every need except the most important...their presence.

Angie Shepard would have given anything to be present for these two perfect little girls, Miranda thought, but life hadn't given her that option. Maybe that's why Miranda didn't mind the barrage of questions. She understood what it was to be left behind.

She knew sometimes little girls simply needed someone there to answer.

"How come some flowers stink?"

"Where's your house?"

"Have you ever been on a rolla coaster?"

"What makes the wind blow?"

"Do you know how to make pancakes?"

"You want us to get you a Popsicle?"

At one point in their chatter, Miranda glanced up and saw a young girl watching from the nearby veranda. She was slightly built, no longer a child, but not quite a young woman yet, either. Her hair, a wild tangle of vivid artificial color, pulled up into a spiky ponytail on one side of her head, was meant to draw attention, to intimidate. Her eyes were a startling, stunning blue-green, her gaze both wary and watchful. But what struck Miranda instantly was the defiant tilt of the chin and the slightly stiff set of the shoulders, a stance that signified both loss and responsibility. She understood that posture, knew without a shared word that Nate's oldest daughter was taking on a role not rightfully hers. Her sympathy went out to the girl. Perhaps because Cate had lost her mother. Maybe just because she'd come outside to check on her sisters.

The twins caught sight of her. "Cate! Hey, Cate! Guess what we're doing?"

The girl, Cate, grinned and was immediately a

different person. "I know what you're doing," she answered confidently. "You're bothering the land-scaper."

"Nana said we could," one twin defended their action.

"You can come and bother her, too," offered the other. "She doesn't mind, do you…" A frown creased the child's freckled nose. "What was your name?"

"Miranda," Miranda said. "And you—" she looked up at Cate of the oddly colored, off-center ponytail "—must be Kali and Kori's big sister."

"I'm Cate," she replied as if that were admission enough.

"I'm happy to meet you, Cate." Miranda dropped her gaze back to the clipboard, reached into the pocket of her jacket for a measuring tape, knowing teenagers talked if and when they wanted to and usually in reverse correlation to any adult attempt to engage them in conversation. Pulling out the tape, she measured the width of a stone bench, its distance from the walkway, its angle from the house, and jotted the figures on her pad. As she straightened, she caught a glimpse of the twins pointing at her as they jumped up and down and tried to mouth some mysterious, and wildly exaggerated, message to their sister. Miranda's glance slid to Cate, who was frowning earnestly at the girls, cautioning them to stop with a roll of her eyes and the up-and-down jerk of her eyebrows.

When she realized Miranda had caught them in the act, her face slid into that you-can't-prove-anything expression teenagers could do so effortlessly and so well. "There used to be lilacs in the garden," Cate said, waving her hand widely and vaguely toward the house, directing Miranda's attention away from the little girls. "Over there, somewhere."

"I was just thinking some lilacs might be nice here." Miranda used the Pentel to point out several dry, dead bramble bushes that flanked three sides of the concrete bench. "What do you think?"

Cate lifted her thin shoulder in a shrug, obviously not wanting to appear too cooperative. "My mother liked lilacs."

"We might consider planting lilacs there, also." Miranda indicated a raised bed, originally built, she guessed, to incorporate the flow of the terrace steps down into the garden. "That way they'd be visible from the other side of the terrace, as well."

Again the shrug. "Anywhere, I guess."

Miranda sketched a couple of uneven circles around her drawing of the stone bench, penciled "lilac bush" inside, sketched in the raised bed, marking it with a question mark. She might prefer tiered beds there instead of the one, and made a note of that possibility also. ''Thank you, Cate.'' She offered a smile, not too big, not too eager. ''It helps me to know what was here before, what flowers you remember.''

Cate sucked in her lower lip, her body angling away, like a bird ready to fly at any untoward movement. ''There were roses, too,'' she offered tentatively.

''Roses!'' Kali—or Kori—said and began bouncing like a floppy-eared bunny. ''Pink roses!''

''Can—we—have—pink—roses?'' Now both girls were bouncing, the words coming in a duplicate staccato. They were dressed alike, their doggy ears flapped up and down in sync, the soles of their sneakers sent out neon-pink sparks with every jump. Even the way the toes of their shoes turned ever so slightly inward as they hopped up and down was identical. Miranda had no experience with that kind of twinship, but she couldn't help thinking that if she were Nate, she'd be strongly encouraging the girls to develop their own identity. Now, before they began to identify themselves as one-half of a whole. It would be relatively easy, too, at this age to convince them to choose a signature color or to wear their hair in different styles. Even something as simple as Kali choosing to wear plaid ribbons in her hair and Kori opting to wear polka dots would do it. Miranda could think of a dozen simple ways to solve this which-twin-is-which dilemma.

But then, no one had asked her to solve it. And no one was likely to. And if she were asked, she'd say no. Likewise, the fact that Cate was concealing fear and longing behind the facade of her attention-grabbing appearance was none of Miranda's business. Cate Shepard was not Miranda's problem. These bouncing, bobbling, identical children, Nate's children, were not her responsibility, either. No matter how much she might dislike having to address them as a unit instead of as two separate individuals.

"If you like pink roses," she said to them now, "then we'll have pink roses."

Their exuberant squeals cartwheeled harmlessly into the blue autumn sky, but their bouncing escalated dramatically, setting them on a collision course with each other. Elbows thumped, knees knocked, feet tangled, and one of them—impossible to know which—stumbled off the path and into the bramble of dry, dead bushes. The other twin, off balance, grappled with gravity and fell in the opposite direction…skidding on her hands and knees across a bed of gravel. Miranda knew immediately it was double trouble, even before their identical banshee wails pierced the cool afternoon air.

Cate was down the steps in an instant, but Miranda was faster, grabbing up one child around the waist, lifting her away from the gravel pit, assessing the best way to get the other one out of the brambles without causing further injury. She sank onto the concrete bench, holding one child in each arm, settling them at cross angles on her lap, comforting them before she even realized what she was doing. She kept up a soothing stream of words, letting the girls cry, offering security and comfort with a caring embrace.

On the walkway, Cate hovered, watching, not coming too close, offering no assistance while Kali and Kori burrowed ever tighter into Miranda's arms, continuing to sob as if their injuries were truly calamitous. At one point, Miranda looked up to see Cate observing her carefully, almost as if judging the way she was handling the situation. Their eyes met and, somehow, Miranda felt she'd passed a test, given the teenager an acceptable answer.

Which was silly. She'd done only what any adult would have done under the circumstances. Okay, so maybe she'd been a little quick to offer aid and sympathy, stepped in to help before she thought. But her response was rooted in her own childhood, in her own experiences of watching out for her little brother and sister. It was grounded in a deeply held belief that when a child scraped her knee or fell into a briar patch, someone should be there to comfort her. It was a natural response, she thought, a desire to feel helpful rather than helpless, a talisman against the fear that somehow she bore some responsibility for the pain, regardless of how it had happened or whose it was.

"Do you have Band-Aids?" she asked Cate. "Maybe some antiseptic cream?"

"In the house." Cate cocked her head to one side, sending the blueberry-colored tip of her ponytail fanning across her pale cheek. "They're getting blood on you."

Miranda looked down to see blood beading along the scratches on Kali's arm, a thin dribble of blood trickling down Kali's leg. Or vice versa. Shifting, she tapped the twin with the scraped elbow on the chin. "Who are you?" she asked. "Kali or Kori?"

"Kali."

The question—one these two probably heard several times a day—was mundane enough to distract them momentarily, and their crying subsided into pitiful snuffling. They turned equally pitiful, tear-streaked faces up to hers. "I got b-blood on your shirt," Kali said with a long-drawn-out sniffle. "I'm-m-m…" Her lower lip began to quiver. "B-b-bleeding."

Kori's lower lip followed suit. "M-m-me, t-too."

Distraction was obviously called for, and Miranda came up with an oldie but goodie. "I think, Kali and Kori," she said slowly, addressing each one in turn, "this qualifies as a two-Popsicle emergency. We'd better go in the house, so we can start the treatment right away."

Their brown eyes—so very much like their father's—brightened and Kori latched on to the defining word. "T-two P-Popsicles?"

Miranda nodded. "Two *each*."

Tears dried like magic. Cate stepped up and took Kali from Miranda, shifting the child onto her hip as if she'd done it a million times before. Miranda gathered Kori against her and stood up from the bench. "If you'll get the Band-Aids, Cate," she said, "Kali and Kori can show me where the Popsicles are stashed."

Cate smiled. A shy, tentative smile. A thank-you smile. A relieved smile. Then she turned toward the house, a thin teenager carrying just one of her sisters up the terrace steps. "Everything's going to be okay now," she said to Kali. Or maybe she was talking to herself. "Everything's going to work out just fine."

Which, when Miranda thought about it, seemed a rather odd thing for a teenager with fluorescent hair to say.

NATE'S HAPPY WHISTLE died in his throat as he turned the corner and saw the big fire truck, red lights flashing, parked in front of his house. A whole gamut of horrible possibilities raced through his mind in the interminable seconds it took for him to pull up to the curb and get out of his SUV. Something could have happened to his mother, to Maggie, to one of the kids. A heart attack. An accident. A disaster. Hurrying, his heart pounding with panic, he rounded the bulk of the fire truck and saw them all, safe and sound, on the front lawn. His mother. Maggie. All four of the kids. Two firefighters in full regalia. And Miranda.

Miranda?

His heart changed rhythm, panic turned into bone-melting relief, and beneath his very genuine concern for his family, he recognized a slow, sweet pleasure at the sight of her. She looked beautiful, her blond hair clasped loosely in a wide, zebra-striped clip. Her clothing seemed different, somehow, the hem of her shirt falling low on her thighs. Just seeing her from the back interfered with his breathing, made him acutely aware of her even in the midst of what was obviously a crisis. She, however, appeared to be an oasis of calm in the middle of a very excited storm. The kids—even Will—were clustered around her, and all three girls were talking fast and furiously, with his mother and Maggie interjecting questions and comments from right behind them. No one noticed his approach because they were all staring at the house, listening to one of the firefighters explain that it would be some time before anyone could go inside.

"What happened?" Nate stopped beside Will and was instantly bombarded by the Kays. They flung themselves at him, shrieking with excitement and overstimulation, trying to leap up and into his arms. "Daddy! Daddy!" they squealed, grabbing for his hand, his arm, a toehold on security. "Guess what? Guess what! There was a fire! A fire!"

"But we 'scaped!"

"Thank God, you're here." His mother frowned at him as if he'd known what awaited him and had purposefully dawdled all the way home to avoid it. "There's been a fire."

"I wasn't even here," Will said, quickly excusing himself from any inherent blame. "I just got back from Cody's house."

"Nobody was hurt," Cate interjected, her eyes cloudy with images of what might have happened.

"That's the important thing," Maggie reminded them all.

Miranda's gaze met his, skimmed away.

"What happened?" Nate asked again, expecting a succinct answer from the firefighters.

But the little girls pounced on the question and buried the hope of a quick, no-nonsense answer.

"It was a two-Popsicle 'mergency, Daddy."

"Look, Daddy, I hurt my knee."

"My arm got all scratch-ed up."

"We saved the Band-Aids, Daddy." One of the Kays held up the Curad box proudly.

"We had Popsicles."

"Two of 'em. Each."

"A grape one and a strawberry one."

Sure enough, Nate could see the evidence in traces of Popsicle purple and red around their mouths.

"Then Miranda showed us what to do with marshmallows."

"Kali burned hers up."

"I did not."

"Did, too."

"Did not."

Nate separated the twins and nipped the budding argument—brought on, no doubt, by more excitement than they normally created over the course of a single day—by laying a hand on top of each head and signaling with slight pressure that he wanted them to be quiet for two seconds. "Let's let the firemen talk," he said. "It's their turn."

The firefighters, once allowed to speak uninterrupted, were quick and to the point. There'd been a fire. Caused, apparently, by burning marshmallows. In the family room. Damaged—a set of drapes, a small section of carpet and a lot of paint. Demolished—a candle and a bag of marshmallows. Verdict—they were lucky it wasn't worse.

"It will be several hours before the smoke clears out," the fireman concluded. "If I were you, I'd find somewhere else to stay tonight. At least send the kids off until tomorrow or the day after."

"Walt Disney World!" One of the Kays shouted, immediately thinking of a good place to be sent.

"Yea! Walt Disney World," seconded the other.

"We are *not,*" Nate said firmly, still not clear on who exactly had been roasting marshmallows and how exactly that had caused the drapes to catch fire, "going to Walt Disney World. We'll go to a hotel."

"I'll stay with Cody," Will promptly stated.

"I'll go to Meghan's house," Cate quickly added.

"Don't worry about Maggie and me," Charleigh announced. "We'll stay with the Parhams. That will be more convenient for us and them, anyway, since we're all flying down together in their private jet. You just manage the children. Maggie and I will take care of ourselves."

The crisis was only now beginning to take the stiffening out of his knees and already his family seemed eager to scatter to the four winds. What had happened to the ties that bind? If Angie had been here, the children wouldn't have been so quick to abandon ship. They would have wanted to stay close, would have found security in the idea of being together. Of course, if Angie were here, no one would have been burning marshmallows in the family room.

"I'll take them to Danfair with me." Miranda's voice was calm, cool and collected, her smile softening the take-charge tone with warm invitation. "It's not Walt Disney World, but it's close. And it's a lot better than a hotel." Her blue eyes turned to Nate. "You can stay here and finish with the fire department. Take all the time you need. We'll see you for dinner, then?"

She made it a question, but he suspected she already knew the answer. There, in that moment of eye contact, they shared an unspoken understanding, a sharing that went deeper than, perhaps, either of them had meant it to go. But there it was. Unspoken understanding. An agreement of purpose. She'd whisk his children off and occupy them elsewhere while he dealt with the practicalities. She'd give them all a chance to level off from the frantic highs of the adrenaline rush, give him the opportunity to see for himself that no true harm had been done, time to deal with the choking fear of what might have happened and to avoid the temptation to over-react that often followed.

And even with that subtext circulating between them in those few seconds of eye contact, he had the most amazing thought that somehow she'd had something to do with the flaming marshmallows. He couldn't imagine how she had come to play such a role in his house, with his children, but looking at her now, seeing the faintest glint of guilt in her eyes, this thought became an elusive suspicion. Whatever had actually happened, he suddenly felt certain there had been *some* adult involvement in this childish prank gone awry. And, if by some as yet unknown fluke, that adult involvement had come from Miranda…well, then, there was more mischief in her than he would ever have suspected.

"Thank you, Miranda," he said, giving away not even a hint of his suspicion. "Danfair, it is." He instructed his children to stifle any and all protests with the *look*.

And when all of his children, from oldest to youngest, rolled their eyes and gave a collective sigh, making fun of his attempt as they always did, he felt that all was right with his world.

Chapter Seven

"Now you've done it."

Nate's voice came out of the darkness behind her, sending a thrill as sleek as silk on skin whispering down her spine. She turned to face him, finding support in the railing that ran along the terrace wall behind her. The night air held a nip of autumn, and she rubbed her hand across her sweater sleeves, the cashmere a soft warmth beneath her fingers. She wasn't chilled, though, and it certainly wasn't the crisp September night that brought a flush to her cheeks. Oh, no, it was the man walking out through the open French doors to join her who was to blame for that.

Blushing. She was blushing. And she was almost thirty. Way past any good explanation for such an age-of-innocence reaction. She couldn't even use the element of surprise as an excuse. She'd known he would seek her out at some point this evening and, as it was now nearly ten-thirty and the evening almost over, she couldn't claim she hadn't been expecting him. She'd even come outside to wait for him, choosing that as preferable to conversing with him under Ainsley's overeager supervision. For the past ten minutes—all right, so really for the entire evening—she had anticipated what he might want to say to her, what she might want to answer, if he might try to kiss her again, if she might let him. But now that he was here, all of those answers, any strategies she'd planned to cope with this attraction, everything, except the delicious anticipation of what could happen, floated up and away from her thoughts like a helium balloon. "Done what?" she asked in a voice she tried to make so deliberately casual it came out almost as a whisper.

"You've upped the ante," he replied in a voice as natural as the way he came to her side and stopped beside her, not too close but close enough for her to feel the warmth of his body, to inhale the faint scent of his aftershave. "In one evening, you've managed to wipe out the appeal of a trip to Walt Disney World in favor of remodeling the Shepard home à la Danfair."

"Your children did seem to like the house."

"Children?" he scoffed. "I was talking about me. What red-blooded American male wouldn't want a pool table in the study, a tournament table-tennis set in the living room and an inline-skating rink in the ballroom? The only thing I'd change would be to make the indoor croquet field into a miniature golf course.''

''Matt and Andy have wanted to do that for years, but there's just too much potential for real damage with miniature golf. So croquet it stays.''

''Well, I suppose even the planners at Walt Disney World had to make a few concessions.''

She smiled, stared at the rectangles of golden light, which spilled from the library and ebbed into the shadows where she and Nate stood, and thought about how her home had evolved into an oddity over the years of her childhood. She and her siblings had often been alone, with plenty of adults about, but no one really in charge and no one to tell them they couldn't put a croquet field in the foyer or that they shouldn't skate on the hardwood floor of the huge old ballroom. They'd played basketball in there, too, until the antique mirror had accidentally cracked on a layup. Even then, there had been no repercussions except for the guilt at breaking something not easily—or ever—replaced.

Perhaps Charles and Linney had felt guilty about being absent so often and that was why they'd allowed their children to turn the house into a playground. But, personally, Miranda thought her parents had never really noticed the changes. They paid so little attention to mundane details, anyway, always focusing on the big picture, on the problems of a world outside the walls of home. It was easy to believe they simply stepped over the croquet mallets and walked around the Ping-Pong table without registering their presence. Matt, on the other hand, had always claimed that their mindful inattention was Charles and Linney's gift to their children. It offered them the freedom to choose. An unquestioned right to make what they wanted of their own lives. Most of the time, Miranda was happy not knowing whether her theory or Matt's lay closer to the truth.

"I sometimes wonder what adults think when they see Danfair for the first time," she mused aloud. "It is an unusual home, to say the least. Matt, the twins and I talk sometimes about changing it back into a more traditional house, but we never do anything about it. Maybe when Matt marries…*if* he marries…the change will take place naturally then."

"I, for one, would be sorry to see that happen." Nate braced his hands on the railing, leaned forward, then rocked back. "Not for Matt to marry, of course, but for the childlike charm of your home to be replaced by layers of untouchable elegance. Give me a house with character any day."

"Not everyone thinks the *character* of this house is worth preserving."

"Don't tell me someone has complained?" He

shook his head. ''When I'm elected and you're re-elected to the city council, let's introduce a city ordinance against frivolous complaining.''

''Don't tell me you're one of those who likes to stir things up,'' she said with a laugh.

''Don't tell me *you're* one of those who likes to maintain the status quo.'' His smile teased her in the soft night lighting. ''I can see it may be a stormy couple of years for the other councilors. On the other hand, you can always count on my support if you invite me over to skate after the meetings.''

The way the moonlight teased a reddish cast into Nate's dark hair fascinated her. ''I'm surprised at you, Nate Shepard. That sort of comment could be construed as blackmail or bribery. You should watch your step. Things like that can get you into a lot of trouble.''

''Things like marshmallows can get you into a lot of trouble,'' he observed blandly. ''Which brings me to the question that's been on my mind since I saw you standing outside my house this afternoon.''

Of course, he'd want an explanation from her. And she shouldn't have made him wait so long for it, either. If she'd been in his place, she wouldn't have been so patient about asking the question. Of course, there had been all manner of explanations from the children already. They'd turned the fire into an entertaining tale, told from different and exaggerated viewpoints, often with wild embellishment, some of it based in fact, some not. "I do feel, at least, partly responsible for what happened this afternoon," she admitted.

His gaze cut to her. His eyebrows quirked upward. An indication that he was willing to listen to her side of the story. The story. What, exactly, had happened? Miranda was still sorting through that and just how much she wanted to confess. "I went to your house to do the landscape assessment," she said, then paused to gather her thoughts.

"I'm relieved to know you didn't go there to burn down my house."

"It was a *very* small fire." She mimicked the arch of his eyebrows and he subsided with a grin.

"Kali and Kori fell. In the garden. Outside." She wanted to be sure he realized she hadn't simply rung his doorbell, gone inside and made herself at home. "Kali scraped her arm and Kori skinned her knee and they both cried pretty hard and I...well, I think that when children are hurting, someone should do something to make them feel better. Your mother had left to run an errand, so I took them inside to clean them up."

"Where was Cate?"

"She was there. Helping. She brought the Band-Aids and the antiseptic cream and some old wash cloths so I could clean the wounds. But, really, she's only a child herself.''

"Don't let her hear you say that.''

"Well, she is, nonetheless, and I hated for her to have the responsibility of distracting her sisters, so I asked her to get them some Popsicles, which she did. From there…well, the marshmallow subject arose when Kali asked if I liked Popsicles when I was their age, which I did. Then Kori wanted to know if I ever liked anything better than Popsicles, to which I should have said no. But I didn't. Then they wanted to know practically everything I'd ever tasted and how it was better than a Popsicle, and before I realized it, I was explaining how Matt and I invented popcorn baseball and the time Ainsley and Andrew decided to make cotton candy in the clothes dryer and—'' She caught his pained expression and added, "Don't worry. I told them it didn't work.''

"But did you tell them who had to clean up the mess?'' he asked. "A much more important point to make at their age.''

She laughed. "Actually, I don't remember who cleaned up that disaster, but the clothes dryer vanished, never to be seen again. My point is, that's how the whole discussion of, and subsequent toasting of, marshmallows came about. The consequence, unfortunately, was the fire. A *small* fire.''

"I'm still not clear on how exactly the flaming marshmallow set the drapes on fire...but on second thought, maybe it's best I don't know too many details."

"Probably best," she agreed. "And I wouldn't say it was *flaming,* although it was definitely on fire."

His low sound of amusement whispered through the night to caress her. "I can see that I have underestimated you, Miranda."

She loved the flirtation in his voice, that husky note of surprise, and knew the sliver of attraction had the potential to become a chasm she could fall into. "What?" she flirted back...recklessly, as it turned out. "You didn't think I'd try something like setting your house on fire to get your attention?"

It was the last thing—the absolute *last* thing—she had meant to say. But now it was out there. And he knew she'd not only noticed his lack of pursuit, she'd been just a little miffed by it. She, who was always so careful, so deliberate in what she chose to say and do, had suddenly blurted out the most indiscreet of her thoughts. She was—*gasp*—turning into her sister!

Nate straightened slowly away from the railing and angled, only slightly, but very effectively, into her space, interfering with both her heart rate and her breathing in one smooth move. "You've had my attention since the salmon incident, Miranda. Believe me, burning down my house is unnecessary."

She drew a shallow breath, and tried to match the touch of humor that edged his smile. "It was a very…small…fire."

"Mmm." His hands touched hers, moved up to her arms. "But you know what they say about small fires."

Don't ask. Do not ask…. "W-what?" It came out in a whisper, barely a puff of air from her constricted throat.

His eyes found hers in the stillness and viewed her with a tender pleasure. He breathed…and she felt the warmth of his amusement on her cheek. "They say, Miranda, that small fires spread and turn into big fires."

She believed that. Her body offered plenty of proof. What had started as a blush of anticipation had already become a simmer of heat beneath her skin. And where his hands rested lightly—so lightly—on the sleeves of her sweater, there was a sizzle of expectation. He intended to kiss her. Again. She felt certain of his intent and knew she ought to have enough pride to put a stop to this, right here, right now. But apparently, her pride had gone the way of her senses, because she only stood, a willing hostage while the fire spread, wanting only to feel the burning touch of his mouth over hers.

Without so much as a cue, her lips parted with invitation and his gaze dropped to trace the nervous path of her tongue as it skimmed her lower lip. She had never been this anxious about a coming kiss, had never before been eager for a man to take the decision out of her hands and kiss her. Yet still he waited. As if this—the anticipation—was the best part, the moment he most wanted to savor.

''Thank you for telling me about the fire,'' he said softly. ''But that wasn't the question I was going to ask you.''

She could hardly breathe for wanting his kiss. ''It...wasn't?''

''No.'' He shook his head. ''The thing that has bothered me all afternoon and all evening is that, when we were all standing out on the lawn while the firefighters put out the fire, I think you were wearing my shirt. Is that possible?''

Her eyelids came down on a sigh and the blush returned to her cheeks in a heated rush. ''Yes,'' she said a moment later. A *long* moment later. ''Yes, I was wearing your shirt.'' How such a simple, perfectly innocent, harmless action could suddenly sound so naughty, confused her. But there it was. She had worn his shirt and somehow, on this starstruck night, the admission felt sinfully intimate. ''I...well, mine had a stain on it and...and I asked Cate to get me something to wear while I rinsed mine out. Then we started roasting the marshmallows and…''

''And the fire started.''

Her sense of pride returned. Late, but welcome. ''I'll have it dry-cleaned and back to you by Monday.''

''Keep it,'' he said. ''I'll never be able to wear the shirt again, knowing it looks so much better on you.''

''You'll have it Monday,'' she promised.

''I can see that this relationship is going to be hard on my wardrobe,'' he went on, ignoring her disclaimer. ''Come to think of it, I'm not sure I have enough shirts for both of us. I think, Miranda, that you and I are going to need to do some shopping.''

She was back and ready for him. Bring it on. Cut to the bottom line. ''What relationship?''

He answered with a slow smile that on another man, a younger man, might have seemed cocky, but on Nate, simply looked confident. ''I do have one other question.''

''Save it for a rainy day,'' she told him, feeling she'd just stepped back from the precipice.

And then Ainsley showed up to push her over the edge.

''Miranda?'' The sound of her footsteps preceded her, but Ainsley, being Ainsley, had never been particularly stealthy. ''Is Nate out there with you?''

As if the *matchmaker* didn't know to the second exactly how long he'd been out here with her. "We were just coming in." Miranda would have moved toward the door then, but his hands were still on her arms, his body between her and the house, and he didn't seem in any hurry to move. "We should go in," she suggested, aware as she said it of a reluctance to leave, the heat of his hands made her want to run with him into the darkness, and discover if there was fire to be found within the kiss he'd denied her.

"We could make a run for it," Nate said, reading her mind.

God help her, she was tempted. "Where would we go?"

"Walt Disney World?"

Ainsley stopped in the doorway, an angel in pale blue. "Oh," she said, heavy on the surprise. "Hi, there. I was looking for you."

Nate's wry expression—all and only for Miranda—made her laugh. She would have taken the initiative then and kissed him as she'd wanted him to kiss her. But she did not want her sister—the *matchmaker*—to see anything remotely *match*-like, and besides, Nate was already stepping back, turning, and placing his hand at her elbow to draw her toward the light along with him. "Miranda and I were just talking about fire safety,'' he said in a tone no twenty-something would ever dare argue with.

This time Ainsley's ''Oh'' was clearly disappointed. But she recovered. ''Well,'' she added brightly, turning to walk with them into the room, ''that's something else the two of you have in common.''

''Fire safety?''

Ainsley nodded. ''Miranda used to give us lectures on stuff like that all the time. Fire safety, auto safety, weather safety, you-name-it safety. She was very strict about safety.''

Miranda was wishing she'd been stricter about talking, when she felt Nate's fingers brush across her hand. She looked up to see a tender regret in his eyes.

''Did you ever get to be a child, Miranda?''

A lump the size of Seattle rose in her throat then. And she had to blink back unexpected tears. No one had ever asked her that question. She'd never even asked it of herself. But Nate saw her sacrifice, acknowledged it, and felt regret on her behalf. As moments go, it was one of the sweetest she'd ever known. She offered him a soft smile in thanks and lifted her shoulder in a light shrug of acceptance. ''Well,'' she said, ''I did invent popcorn baseball.''

''Oh, and that's not all.'' Ainsley—as matchmaker—seemed intent on cataloging Miranda's many achievements for Nate, chattering on about other games, other perfectly *brilliant* ideas Miranda had had over the years. She kept up a continuous stream of cute stories as the three of them walked through the study, past the game-filled dining room, crossed the croquet field, and skirted the Ping-Pong table into the East Salon.

And all the while, Nate listened politely, while behind Ainsley's back, his fingers flirted outrageously with Miranda's.

It wasn't a kiss, but it had promise. Small fires, Miranda thought, gave off a surprising amount of warmth.

"MOMMY!"

Miranda was out of bed and halfway down the hall before she became fully awake and understood the cry in the night was not for her. It had been years—a great many of them—since she'd awakened to a child's frightened call. Ainsley had often cried out in her sleep whenever their parents were away...and she wouldn't let anyone but Miranda comfort her. Andrew, too, had gone through times when he awoke sobbing and Miranda had been the only one who could soothe him. If Matthew had ever had nightmares, he'd never let her know. But then, he was older and had always felt he needed to be the man of the family. Just as she'd always felt it was her duty to be the mother they so seldom saw.

That had been a long time ago, when she was only a child herself and she'd thought it was mostly forgotten. Until now, all these years later, when she was here again, in the middle of the night, out of bed, called out of sleep, on her way to another bedside, responding to someone else's need without a second—or a first—thought. Miranda to the rescue, hurrying to dispel unfounded fears, conditioned by her own deep sense of responsibility to find the problem and fix it. Even when it wasn't her problem.

The crying was muted now, no longer the frantic, frightened call of a child waking from a bad dream and into strange surroundings. Miranda told herself to turn around and go back to bed. Nate and his children were all in guest rooms, situated close together. He would have heard the cry and responded. He was their father. Any calls were his to answer. Not hers. And yet, she continued quietly padding barefoot down the hall toward the doorway of the room Kali and Kori were sharing for the night. Just to check. Just to make sure someone had heard. Just to settle her own restless worry.

How many times had she made this same journey through the halls of Danfair to the bedside of a child not her own? It felt so familiar, perhaps it had been hundreds of times. Maybe only a handful. Probably somewhere in between. She had always gone, but she had dreaded the trip. Or, more truthfully, the feeling of great helplessness that accompanied it. She hadn't been sure what was expected, had no way of ever knowing if she'd done what her parents would have done in her place. And afterward, she'd always returned to her own bed, alone and unsettled, wondering if there would ever be anyone to comfort her.

That must be the reason she kept walking now, stopping in the doorway of the guest room only when she saw that Nate was there, already providing the security his child needed. Which was just as it should be. Just as she had hoped it would be. Kali and Kori had lost a mother, but they still had a father who loved them enough to be present, who was just down the hall when they awoke crying in the night. That, Miranda thought, must be a nice feeling.

"Shh." Nate sat on the edge of the bed, soothing his daughter with the low crooning sound of his voice, allaying her fears by simply stroking his hand across her tousled hair. "Shh, Kali," he murmured. "You're okay. We're at Miranda's house, remember? Shh. Daddy's here and you're all right. Everything is all right."

Miranda leaned her shoulder against the door frame, hugging her body with arms that felt suddenly cool and empty. Which was ridiculous. She didn't want a child to look to her for comfort, didn't want anything remotely resembling that kind of responsibility. Not again. And yet, she continued to stand there, observing the scene, admiring the calm, sure way Nate dealt with it, feeling a trace of irrational envy for the confidence he so easily conveyed. He was compassionate, understanding, caring, but also firm in his insistence that the child stay in bed, that she try to go back to sleep, that she believe the nightmare was gone and would not return. He didn't make promises, didn't offer empty platitudes, and he didn't deny Kali her right to be afraid. It was, after all, a scary world and she had lost a blanket of maternal security that couldn't be replaced. But in those few minutes of watching Nate, Miranda realized he was offering the next best thing—his presence and the knowledge that however horrible the dream or the fear of what might be hiding in the dark, it didn't have to be faced alone. Perhaps the comfort he offered—a loving touch, the murmur of a familiar voice, the relief of having someone come when you called—was the only comfort to be found in the night. Perhaps it was the only comfort a child, or anyone else, really wanted. And maybe, all those years ago, she had unknowingly and however uncertainly, provided the one thing her little family truly needed from her…the gift of not being alone.

Nate looked back and saw her, sharing with her

in that unguarded moment something she hadn't meant to share. She hadn't wanted to see herself as needing comfort, hadn't wanted him to see her that vulnerable. But for the space of a heartbeat, she knew he had seen, knew she had allowed him to see, and she understood that simply by standing in the doorway, she was offering comfort to him. And receiving it from him in return. These were his children. She didn't want the responsibility of caring for another set of motherless children, and had no intention of letting this lovely little flirtation go that far. So why was she standing here, feeling as if she belonged? As if she finally knew what to do?

He rose from the bedside, tucked the covers tightly, securely around the child, kissed her forehead, then turned and came to Miranda. He was half-dressed, wearing a pair of long flannel pants—air force blue—and nothing else. No shoes, no shirt, the feathering of hair across his chest providing the only coverage from the waist up. His dark hair was disheveled, his eyes still somewhat shadowed with sleep, and there were marks on his stubbled jaw, wrinkles imprinted from the sheets onto his skin while he slept. She found that a tender thought for some reason, loved the idea of him sleeping with the linen crumpled up beneath his face.

Nate was a very attractive man...even when not at his best.

Or perhaps, this was the best. No illusions. No pretense. A man, fresh out of bed, awakened with a start—as she had been—and uncaring that she saw him unshaven and unkempt. Or that she was seeing him that way.

Fast on the heels of that thought came the realization that she hardly looked her best. Her nightshirt wasn't sexy or sheer and bordered on the threadbare side of comfort, but it was—no getting around it— short and thin and definitely meant for sleep rather than seduction. Not that she wanted to be wearing anything alluring, but she did wish she had on something a little more, well…feminine…than this faded blue nightshirt with its faded silver moons. A thick, fluffy, long robe would have been nice. But she hadn't thought about that or this, either.

This being she in her nightshirt, standing reasonably close to him in his lounge pants.

She suddenly became excruciatingly aware that between them, they barely had on one pair of pajamas.

"I'm sorry she woke you," Nate said, drawing Miranda out into the hall, his hand on her arm warming her through in just that tiny bit of a minute. "She's done this off and on for a long time. She won't even remember it tomorrow. Most of the time I'm pretty sure she never even completely wakes up."

Nate smiled at her. A sleepy sort of smile. A smile that, for some completely bizarre reason, made her want to giggle. And she *never* giggled, refused to giggle, was way past the age when giggling was even remotely something she would do. On the other hand, she was standing in the hall in her nightshirt talking to a man in his pajamas. She would have thought that wasn't a thing she would do, either. And it probably required some explanation. "I only came to check because I was afraid you might not hear her."

"I may not know what to do with my children in the daylight, but I've been getting up with them in the middle of the night for years now. Thirteen years, to be exact. Ever since we brought Will and Cate home from the hospital. Angie wouldn't have heard a bass drum if I'd been playing it in the bed next to her." His smile softened. "And there were plenty of nights I thought about trying it, too. Just to be sure."

"You're exaggerating," Miranda corrected him, defending a woman she'd never even met. "I can see that you're a wonderful father, but I find it a little hard to believe you were a nighttime martyr."

"Okay, so she took the occasional midnight duty, mostly when I had to be away on deployment. But for the most part, I was the middle-of-the-night designated parent."

And now, she thought, that was his status 24-7.

They stood for a moment, designated parents past and present, and the silence stretched between them, no more noticeable than if it were simply another shadow in the dark. He didn't seem bothered that she wasn't dressed for conversation. He didn't seem to be aware that she was barely dressed. She, on the other hand, felt supremely conscious of being in her nightshirt, completely bewildered at her desire to linger here in the hallway with him, hoping for something she hadn't thought she wanted to happen.

"You know, Miranda," he said after a space that might have been long, might have been brief, "I've been thinking we should take a trip. Maybe next week. If you're free."

"A trip? Together?" Images tumbled through her mind. She and Nate in a car. On a plane. Maybe on a train. A trip to somewhere not here. Time to talk. To laugh. To find the kiss that had earlier eluded them, but still hovered, unfulfilled, between them. "What kind of a...trip?"

"A shopping trip," he said matter-of-factly. "To get some furniture for the coffeehouse. If I take the kids, I'll only wind up with some god-awful, uncomfortable, and probably very purple furnishings not fit for anyone over the age of fifteen. I need help, Miranda. I need your help. Otherwise it could get very ugly."

She was disappointed. And she knew he caught a glimpse of it in her eyes, even though she dropped her gaze hastily to hide the emotion. "I don't really have any time," she said quickly, the words tumbling out in a rush of self-defense. "With Ainsley's wedding, there's so much to do, so many details I need to handle. I just don't see how I can fit anything else in." She forced her gaze up to meet his, hoped it was appropriately apologetic. "You understand."

The corners of his eyes crinkled with a slow, sexy smile. "What I understand—the *only* thing I understand right now—is that trying to talk under these circumstances is a lost cause."

"Circumstances?" she whispered.

He didn't answer, but his expression told her exactly what he meant and, with a bare sigh, she stopped pretending she didn't understand. He was aware of what her nightshirt did...and didn't... cover.The realization made her both self-conscious and flooded her body with a perfectly ridiculous pleasure.

"Much as I hate to suggest this, Miranda, I think you should go back to bed."

There was an inherent choice in the suggestion and, as her eyes met his in the shadowy darkness, she knew they were both imagining the alternative. For a heartbeat, maybe two, she thought about letting it happen, about making it happen. But that was a line she wasn't going to cross. She would go to bed, alone, as would he, even though the thought of him would now go with her as, she was certain, he would take the thought of her with him. Anticipation fairly sparkled in the air between them, making the breath catch in her throat, awakening possibilities throughout her body. "Yes," she said, trying to pull herself away from temptation, even though her feet firmly refused to budge. "I should go to bed."

"Yes," he agreed. "Me, too."

"You are the designated parent."

"And you have a couple of husky brothers just down the hall."

Her smile curved, unbidden. She should not be doing this, had no business enjoying this flirtation. Encouraging it. But she couldn't seem to help herself. The night and Nate were conspiring against her, shutting out her better judgment, trapping her in a delicious fantasy. "They're not so husky," she said.

"I could outrun them, but I'd probably just trip myself up in the croquet field."

She tilted her head to one side, allowed her smile to tease him just a little. "I'm pretty good at first aid."

His eyes burned her with a tender, impossible desire. "Go to bed, Miranda. I'll see you in the morning."

It wasn't rejection. She knew that. She did. But she couldn't stop the wave of disappointment that flooded through her, couldn't keep her gaze from dropping. "I have an appointment. Early. So I probably won't see you...." Her voice faded away because she knew it betrayed her attempt at nonchalance.

"Yes, you will. Now, go."

She knew it was good advice, however reluctant she was to take it. "Nate," she began, not even knowing what she wanted to say.

With a soft sigh, he brought his hand to the back of her head, pulled her to him and took her lips in a long, lovely kiss. A kiss of languid desire and banked passions. A kiss that stole her heart and made no promise to return it. A kiss that made her knees weak. A kiss that set her body trembling beneath the yearning in it. A kiss that...ended and left her wanting more.

So much more.

Nate set her away from him. Firmly. Decisively. Even though his breath was ragged from the effort. "We're not doing this, Miranda. Not tonight. Not here. Not this way. Go to bed. Please."

She opened her mouth to deny that this was happening, to assure him she had no intention of seducing him. Or of allowing him to seduce her. Tonight. Here. This way. Or any other way.

But the look in his dark eyes stopped her from speaking the lie aloud.

"Go," he repeated.

And she went.

Chapter Eight

"Where's Miranda?" Andrew walked into the morning room, where the Danville siblings had gathered for breakfast as long as they could remember, and went straight to the sidebar. "I need to talk to her about the design for tomorrow's photo shoot."

Ainsley glanced up from the society page of the newspaper to assess her twin with a critical eye. Dressed in jeans and a dark sweater, he was the more rugged of her brothers. Matthew was, technically, the more handsome and definitely the more sophisticated, but Andrew's strawberry-blond hair and casual, outdoorsy style gave him an edgy sort of attraction. Of course, he was her twin and she might be—however slightly—biased in his favor. "Andrew?" she mused aloud. "Do you know Peyton O'Reilly?"

"I don't know. Is she pretty?"

"Yes, and new in Newport. Her family bought the Wright mansion and completely tore it apart renovating it. At least, that's what Lucinda told me...and she usually knows."

"Blond or brunette?"

"Lucinda?"

"This Peyton person."

"Oh. Brunette. A very striking brunette. I've been working with her at the pediatric center. She volunteers."

Andrew filled his plate as if second helpings wouldn't be allowed. "Why?"

"She's very committed to helping others, says her parents were very lucky in their business ventures and she believes good fortune must be shared."

"Gee, where have I heard *that* philosophy before?"

"Gee, I can't imagine." Ainsley watched him take a seat at the table and pondered the metabolism that allowed him to eat like a veritable machine and stay lean and muscular as an athlete. "Mom and Dad are going to love Peyton."

"They love anyone who volunteers through the Foundation."

"Yes, but she's...special. They're going to especially love her."

Andrew glanced up with a frown. "This is beginning to sound ominous for someone. Please tell me you're matchmaking for Matt and not for me.''

Ainsley mimicked his frown, exaggerated it, returned it, and told herself she would have to be more careful about what she said around here. Of course, soon—barely four weeks now left until the wedding—she'd be married and living with Ivan. Then her brothers wouldn't constantly think she was trying to set them up with the right woman and an *introduction of possibilities*. Which maybe she was, and maybe she wasn't. ''I'm not matchmaking for you, that's for sure. I'd never be able to find a woman who'd put up with you. How's Hayley?''

''Who?''

''Hayley Sayers? She is still your photography assistant, isn't she?''

He paused for the barest of moments. If she hadn't been watching, she'd have missed it. ''Hayley,'' he repeated, as if trying to place her, ''yes, she's still with me.''

''Really.'' Ainsley knew this was a long shot, but she went for it, anyway. ''How's that going?''

Andrew's gaze cut to Ainsley with suspicion as he reached for the pepper. ''We ignore each other as much as possible. It seems to work better for both of us that way.''

''Hmm,'' Ainsley murmured.

He pointed his fork at her for emphasis. ''Don't

even think about it, Ainsley. Never in a million years will I have more than a professional interest in Hayley Sayers. So just turn your little fairy godmother wand away from me and focus on Matt. He needs a woman to take care of him, especially since Miranda seems to have gone AWOL.''

''She's busy,'' Ainsley said diplomatically, leaving the subject of Hayley for another day.

''I see that cute little glint in your eye, Baby. You're trying to set her up, too, aren't you?''

''Trying to set who up?'' Matt walked into the room in time to overhear the tail end of the conversation.

''No one.'' Ainsley hoped to divert the question with another question. ''You know Peyton O'Reilly, don't you, Matt?''

''Yes, and if she's your next target for matrimony, more power to you. Although I will feel exceedingly sorry for the guy who winds up with her.'' He poured himself a cup of coffee and came to the table. Matt always did meals, and most everything else, in steps. He didn't like to rush. Ainsley admired that, wished she could be less impulsive, more deliberate. But Ivan said she was perfect the way she was, so maybe it was Matt who needed to be a little impulsive.

''Miss O'Reilly,'' Matt continued, ''has been a pain in my side since the first day she showed up at the Foundation and signed up for the volunteer program.''

''She's perfectly lovely, Matt,'' Ainsley protested. ''I've been working with her all summer and I like her very much. You'd like her, too, if you'd take the time to talk to her.''

''I talk about her more than I want to already. She seems to have a way of annoying the other volunteers with her little *projects.*''

''She's eager, that's all.''

Andrew paused in his manly efforts to polish off the first round of breakfast and gave his twin a calculating look. ''Mom and Dad would like her.''

Ainsley lifted her chin, not giving anything away. She hoped. ''Peyton's doing a great job in organizing the Black and White Ball, Matt. I think it's going to be one of the best we've ever had.''

''And it's too late to replace her.'' Matt took a sip of his coffee and reached for the front page of the paper. ''Which is the only reason I haven't passed along the complaints to her. I'm afraid she'll get her feelings hurt and quit. Then I'd have to find someone else to organize the fund-raiser. Or talk Miranda into doing it.''

''Don't even think about asking her.''

Matt flicked the paper into a comfortable reading position. ''Miranda loves challenges. She likes nothing better than to step into a project someone else has abandoned. That's her idea of fun. Where is she, by the way?"

"As it happens, that was the question on the table when you came in. This is the third morning this week she's missed breakfast." Andrew pushed back his chair and made a second trip to the sideboard, casting a sly glance over his shoulder. "Baby was just about to expound on the *possibilities*. Weren't you, Ains?"

Honestly, some days—every day, really—she was so looking forward to her wedding. "Our sister is out having a life of her own. Finally," she said.

Andrew laughed.

Matt smiled. "Where is she really?" he asked.

"She's gone to the Cape for a couple of days," Ainsley replied, thinking her brothers took her sister too much for granted and deserved to be startled out of their complacency. "With Nate Shepard."

Matthew put down the newspaper. Andrew brought his plate—full, again—back to the table. They both looked at Ainsley expectantly.

She waited them out.

"Has she ever taken a man to the beach house before?" Matt posed this question to Andrew.

"Not that I know of," came the answer. "And he did spend the night here, with his kids, last weekend." Andrew looked again at Ainsley. "Did they take his kids?"

Her brothers were so unimaginative. They saw Miranda as a sister, a helpful overseer, the organizer of everyday details in their lives. And were they in for a rude awakening if—*when*—this match worked out. Which was looking more and more possible to Ainsley's practiced eye. "I believe Nate's children are in school and he does have a nanny for them, so no, I imagine Nate and Miranda are alone. And it isn't as if he spent the night here *with* her. There was a fire, you know."

"A little more than that, apparently." Matt frowned. "Did you have anything to do with this, Ainsley?"

"With what?"

"The trip to the beach house."

"No," she said defensively. Although that part, at least, was true. Miranda hadn't consulted her. Not as a matchmaker, which was the way Matt saw it. Not as a sister, which was the way Ainsley wished she might have been consulted. Miranda had simply walked into Ainsley's bedroom the night before and told her she'd be leaving early the next morning and would be away overnight. Possibly longer. She'd seemed rather tense about it, too, but Ainsley had known better than to comment on that. And, as she'd already had a phone call from Cate Shepard, giving her the lowdown from that end, she'd already figured out something was up. Nate, of course, had simply told his children he was going to buy the furniture for the coffeehouse. But from Miranda's jumpy mood ever since the fire, it wasn't hard to read a different agenda into this sudden buying trip.

And Ainsley *was* a matchmaker. Her mind ran along a romantic track on a daily basis. "They're going to buy some furniture for his coffeehouse," she said as if there couldn't possibly be any other reason for the trip to the Cape. Which could be true. Even a full-fledged matchmaker wouldn't have been able to predict the course of the relationship. As Ilsa was fond of saying, once the possibilities had been set in motion, the only thing left to do was step back and observe what happened. "It's business."

And, hopefully, pleasure as well.

"Oh, well, why didn't you say so?" Andrew's appetite returned. "I thought for a minute Miranda was hooking up with the old guy."

"He's not that old."

"He's older than Matt."

"And he has children." Matt raised his coffee cup and returned his attention to the newspaper. "Miranda doesn't want to have children of her own, much less someone else's."

"Who said?" Ainsley asked, wondering where Matt had gotten that idea. Just because *he'd* always claimed not to want marriage or a family didn't mean Miranda felt that way. "Has she ever said that?"

"Yes," Matt replied.

"Only all the time." Realizing he'd forgotten to refill his glass, Andrew reached across and swiped Ainsley's orange juice. "But if she's just helping him get the coffeehouse set up, then that's all right. Bad timing for you, though, Baby."

Ainsley got up, walked to the door between the morning room and the kitchen, and asked their houseboy—a new trainee, only recently arrived at Danfair—to bring out some more orange juice. "Why bad timing for me?" she asked when she was seated again. "Miranda being gone for a couple of days doesn't affect me."

"The wedding," Andrew explained. "I thought she'd be systematically ironing out the details for your wedding instead of taking on a new project. You know how involved she gets in whatever she's doing and, contrary to her belief that she can do twenty things at once, all of them perfectly, she does have her limitations."

"Oh, that," Ainsley said with a laugh. "She's already given me lists of last-minute details I need to take care of, and it's only a wedding. What could possibly go wrong?"

MIRANDA KNEW how to plan a wedding. She knew how to design a garden that would take a viewer's breath away. She knew how to pull separate elements into a whole. She had an eye for color, a flare for design. She was great at prioritizing, organizing and setting agendas. Give her a notepad and a pencil and she could plot out a plan for doing almost anything.

But she didn't have a clue how to plan a seduction.

It had taken her just twenty-four hours after that kiss in the hallway, after Nate had sent her to bed alone, to reach the conclusion that seduction was her best option. Denying the attraction seemed pointless. Every time he came near her, she melted into a rather obvious puddle of willingness. Avoiding him would be childish, requiring evasive tactics she had neither the energy nor patience to carry out. Telling him openly and honestly that she wasn't interested in a relationship with him would only be a lie…and one he'd undoubtedly call her on.

She hadn't felt this out of control for a long time. A very long time. And never with a man.

Except maybe once.

Nate's brother, Nick, had held a mysteriously magnetic attraction for her. Of course, she'd been a teenager and he'd been gorgeous, even then. And charming. And able to sound so convincing, Miranda had long since forgiven herself for falling for his lines. It had been no surprise to her he'd become a successful actor.

After Nicky, though, she'd always maintained a level head, never losing control, never falling further into love than she wanted. Which was probably why her relationships with men, for the most part, had been relatively harmless. A few months of dating, some laughs, some meaningful moments, but ultimately nothing she was ready to move heaven and earth to keep. Even when she'd found a man she thought she could love enough to marry, she hadn't surrendered the piece of herself that needed to be in charge. And when their engagement ended, she was wounded, but not truly grief-stricken. Maybe she had felt she couldn't commit to a family of her own when she was still the centerpiece of the family she had. Maybe she'd just been afraid to take the risk that, when push came to shove, her sister and brothers could—and would—do quite nicely without her. Whatever the foundation of her decision, she'd always felt serene confidence in knowing she had the power to decide how far things went, when and where they stopped.

And that's how it would have to be with Nate.

Even if he did have a strangely debilitating effect on her resolve.

A strangely familiar effect.

Nicky Shepard had been her first tryst with love. With lust, more aptly. A rush of teenage hormones mixed with poor judgment on her part, raw sexual appeal on his. Not that their great love affair had ever progressed beyond a few—okay, a lot of—hot, exploratory kisses and a good deal of frustration. She'd spent most of her time corralling his roving hands, while he'd spent his testing to see what else he could get away with. They'd been teens and without much sense of the trouble they were courting, but somehow Miranda had managed to pull back from the promise of passion and the lack of control it exercised over her. She hadn't liked that restless, reckless feeling and she'd never let things get so heated since.

Until now…when with a few practiced kisses—and not a single instance of roving hands—Nate made her remember the exhilaration of that first, breathtaking experience. He made her think letting go was desirable, that surrendering control would bring pleasure, that acquiescence offered sweet freedom from responsibility. She recognized that temptation, the soft enticement of it, and felt its seductive power even now. Except she was older, smarter, no longer a curious, clueless teen. She had learned that in this game of attraction, someone had to take charge.

And, if there was one thing Miranda knew, it was how to be in charge.

So she would use the attraction to put an end to the speculation on her part that this ''thing'' with Nate was any more dangerous than the fleeting desire she'd once felt for his brother. No more, no less. So if a relationship *was* going to develop—and she had admitted the appeal of that possibility to herself within the contemplation of those twenty-four hours—then the only question, in her mind, was who defined the terms. And as allowing Nate to decide when, where and how far things went seemed unpredictable and could prove hazardous, she meant to avert disaster by taking charge of their affair.

Affair.

The very thought of it had her trembling. Which had never happened to her before and was not conducive to forming a plan. She needed a plan. An outline for seduction. A time. A place. The right atmosphere. A list.

She needed a list.

1. Place
   a) Private
   b) Romantic
   c) Within driving distance of home

2. Day/Time
   a) Overnight?
   (Yes, definitely. Expecting less smacks of no courage!)

3. Amenities
   a) Fresh linens
   b) Lingerie (sexy or simply nice?)
      a. Do not want to appear overeager
      b. Shopping?
   c) Food
      a. Convenient
      (Too much preparation suggests nervous-
      ness)
      b. Crackers/cheese (?)
      c. Nate might prefer clams
   d) Wine (Cabernet or a nice Riesling)
      a. Corkscrew (in case we're away from the
      house)
      b. Wineglasses (same reason)
   e) Music
      a. Take CDs—not Bee Gees
      b. Classical, perhaps
   f) Flowers
      a. Ask Teresa (cottage housekeeper) to arrange

4. Necessities (!!)
   a) Protection
   b) Protection
   c) Protection

THE LIST SEEMED woefully inadequate, however, when Nate—all six foot something of him—was scrunched beside her in the snug interior of her little

Mercedes. The idea was hers, so it was only fair that she should drive. At least, that's what she'd told him when she suggested this buying trip. He hadn't seemed to mind, had simply seemed happy that she had agreed to help him find some suitable furnishings for the coffeehouse. If he noticed her distracted attempts at normal conversation, he didn't let on. They'd talked, of course—she wasn't completely stifled by nerves!—about the coffeehouse and possible contemporary stylings they might consider, places he'd lived, places she'd visited, his mother, her parents, his children, her brothers, Ainsley. Nate was easy to talk to, interesting and interested, intelligent and thoughtful, as eager to know her opinions as to express his own. But the really amazing thing to Miranda was that he seemed just as comfortable, just as easy, whether it was conversation or silence that ebbed and flowed between them. Nate was, simply, good company.

They spent the morning in Boston, looking at some of the more modernistic pieces she thought might work in the coffeehouse, ordered three S-shaped sofas—one in red, one in lavender, one an odd green-gold color—five mosaic tables with chairs, a dozen overstuffed chairs in various stripes and patterns, and a black-and-white-tiled oblong bar. Nate thought of adding ornamental track lighting, and they spent an hour debating the right size and shape. They ate a late lunch and headed for Cape Cod, where they arrived to find the art gallery she preferred already closed for the day. Sticking to her plan despite a surfeit of doubts, Miranda asked if Nate would mind stopping at the family beach house before going back to Newport. He'd given her an odd, questioning look at that point, one she didn't allow herself to analyze, but she'd gone on, ignoring the question in his eyes, airily chatting about checking on the house, about the times…few though they had been…when her family had used the house and spent a day or two at the Cape.

"Andy loves it here." Miranda unlocked the door and threw it open, inviting Nate inside. "He has ever since he was a little guy. I don't know why, exactly. It doesn't have any of the kid appeal of Danfair, and while the view here is nice, we do have a pretty spectacular one at home." She closed the door, allowing the intimacy of the cottage to surround them, hoping the seclusion would begin to ease her tension. "But Andrew loves it and comes here quite a lot on his own. More than the rest of us of put together. I'm not sure if it's the scenic photo ops around Cape Cod Bay or the solitude of the house itself that appeals most to him."

Nate didn't comment, just looked around the open living, dining and kitchen area with obvious interest.

"Mom inherited this house from her grandfather,'' Miranda continued. ''I think that's probably the only reason we still have it. My mother isn't sentimental about a lot of things. And, of course, Andrew would have a fit if they tried to sell it. This will probably be his one day. He's the obvious one to have it. The only one of us, really, who genuinely loves being here.''

''I'm surprised you don't like it, Miranda,'' Nate said, giving her an odd look. Sort of like the earlier odd look, but different, too. ''This seems like the perfect place to relax and escape from your responsibilities for a while.''

Her laugh sounded nervous even to her own ears. ''I'm not into escape,'' she responded blithely. ''I'm too practical for the beach house and I almost never relax.''

The curve of his smile chided her softly. ''All the more reason to grab a few stolen hours by the sea when the opportunity arises. Relaxation is a state of mind, you know. One that is well worth learning.''

''Did they teach you that in the air force?''

''No, Angie taught me that.''

''Was she good at it?''

''Relaxing?'' He shook his head. ''No, she was terrible at it. Never still, never satisfied unless she was up and doing something. But when she got sick, time became the enemy, began running out faster than we could catch it, and she had to learn to be quiet, to rest. Just sitting with her taught me the intrinsic value of living in the moment.'' His gaze caught hers, held it. "Close your eyes, Miranda," he said. "Listen. Feel the quiet."

Obediently, her eyes closed. She listened. *The sound of the water lapping against the piers outside. The creak of wood grown old around her. The thud-thud beating of her heart.* She felt. *The cool air off the bay seeping past the windows and into the house. The familiar yearning for unity and connection...all of her family around her, mother, father, sister, brothers, the grandfather she barely remembered, the grandmother she had never known.* She opened her eyes...and Nate was there, waiting.

"Good?" he asked.

"Nice," she answered. "But as for living in the moment, I think I trust the noisy moments more than I do the peaceful ones."

His smile slipped past her boundaries, into her heart. "So do I," he admitted. "Most of the time. And *that* I learned from my kids."

A shiver of anticipation slipped down her spine. She wanted this...wanted *him* more than she had let herself believe. Which seemed suddenly a scary thing.

"This is nice." He ran his hand across the slatted back of a chair, a chair that was older than them both. "Maybe we should have designed the coffeehouse with this cozy, beachy feel instead of going for the art deco look.''

"You can call and cancel the furniture orders," she said. "But I warn you, beach-house chic will require more painting."

"No purple walls?"

"A softer shade, anyway."

"A romantic lavender instead of the passionate grape we now have, you mean."

Her gaze followed his long fingers as he stroked the burled wood and a knot of apprehension budded in her throat. She didn't have the courage to do this. What if the attraction was all in her head? What if he was surprised and unreceptive to her ideas of seduction? What if all her planning offended him?

This was not a good idea. This was too calculating, too planned, too…risky. What had she been thinking? Believing she could be in charge of something as unpredictable as another person's feelings. This was wrong. She'd been wrong. Not everything could…or should…be done with a list.

"Everything looks great," she said brightly, not having moved from the door. "We can go now. I can tell Andrew I checked and everything was fine. Just fine. Of course, we have someone who takes care of the house. But he wanted me to check while I was close. So now I have." She wouldn't look at Nate. Couldn't, as she reached behind her, grasped the doorknob, thought she might just escape unscathed. "Are you ready?"

The pause was pregnant, the room flooded with a soft, strange tension. "Should we…take the flowers?" he asked slowly.

Flowers. Fresh flowers. Put there, at her request, by Teresa, the woman who looked after the cottage.

"Seems a shame to let something so beautiful die unappreciated and alone," he added.

She lifted her chin, fought to maintain a nonchalant smile, but her gaze touched his, turned cowardly and skittered to the bouquet. From the corner of her eye, she saw him make a slight sweep of one hand.

"It seems to me," he continued in a considering tone, "the reason that corkscrew and those two wineglasses were left out on the counter is because there's a bottle of wine around here somewhere. And I have this crazy idea that if I snapped my fingers, the lights would dim and the music would start playing."

Miranda sighed, reluctantly met his eyes straight-on, noted the trace of humor in their whiskey-colored depths. Caught. And only inches from an exit, too.

"I don't know about you, Miranda, but I think your brother may be using the family cottage as a…a love nest."

Sometimes—not often, but definitely now—she

wished she didn't pay such close attention to detail. "The flowers do tend to indicate a certain premeditation, don't they?"

His nod was solemn as he walked into the kitchen, opened the refrigerator, found the wine. "Mmm," he said over his shoulder. "A Riesling. Nice."

It was better than nice. Exquisite. Extra dry. Exotic. She knew because she'd chosen the vintage herself, had it sent ahead. "Oh," she said. "Hmm."

"There's cheese in here, too. Chilled shrimp. Something chocolate. This is a scene set for seduction, no doubt about it." He closed the refrigerator door, raised his eyebrows at her, moved around the breakfast bar and down the hall...where she knew he'd see the bed, freshly made, turned down, ready for action.

Humiliation rose like a flag in her cheeks. *Guilty,* it waved. *Guilty of unfettered planning. Guilty of thinking she could manipulate something as tempestuous as lust. Guilty of overthinking what naturally could have happened so simply.* How had she believed, even for a second, this would work?

Nate returned. "You shouldn't go in there," he said, indicating the bedroom down the hall. "Not alone, anyway. I'm afraid it confirms our suspicions."

"It does?"

"The sheets are satin. Red satin."

That had not been on the list. She would be talking to Teresa about that particular detail for sure. She cleared her throat, found it easy to look appalled. "Andrew has always had abysmal taste in bed linens."

"Oh, I don't know," Nate said, coming closer. "I think they show his artistic bent…and a willingness to live on the edge."

"I hardly think sheets can offer any deep insight."

He stopped in front of her. He didn't touch her, but then, he didn't really need to. She was trembling already at the thought that he might. "I disagree," he said. "I think sheets can be very revealing."

She made a futile attempt to hold her ground. "I had nothing to do with those sheets, Nate."

He lifted his eyebrows in a question, but his eyes offered a warm, sure encouragement.

No guts, no glory, she thought with a sigh. "I *might* have asked Teresa to change the bed linens," she admitted. "But I swear I didn't know about the satin sheets."

"What about the wine? The cheese? The chocolate?"

"It's possible Andrew keeps the refrigerator stocked, the glasses out and ready."

He nodded. "I imagine he could have a standing order for fresh flowers, too. Just in case."

The blush fanned out across her cheeks in a rosy warmth. "I...I *might* have ordered those, myself."

"I hope you did, Miranda. I sincerely hope that you did." He reached up, tenderly stroked her cheek with roughly textured knuckles. "Because I've never slept on satin sheets before and I've always thought I'd like it."

"I don't know why," she said, practicality reasserting itself. "Satin is very cool to the touch. And too slick for comfortable sleep."

"I wasn't, entirely, thinking about sleeping."

"Oh." The tension snapped to attention, wove like a soft scent between them. "Well, in that case, I *might* have arranged for the wine and the food, as well. Would you like some?"

"Oh, yes," he replied, desire appearing first within the golden flecks of his eyes, before it touched his lips and drew his smile into a solemn, settled line. "Later." His hands slid around her waist, drew her unresisting body against him. "And, just so you know, Miranda. I'd have been more than flattered if all you'd done was remember to bring the key."

His nearness made it impossible to think. The moment surrounded her, as elusive as the sound of the surf outside, as sweet as a baby's sigh. "I've carried the key in my purse all week,'' she confessed, feeling he deserved to know.

The look he gave her melted the starch in her knees, brought her hands slipping possessively up his chest, raised her lips to meet his kiss, had her breathless with yearning. A restless urgency tangled with years of carefully honed control and came out the victor. Deep inside her, nerves tightened, flowered with hope. Her body craved the intimacy of his touch, her skin flushed with expectation. Eagerness pulsed through her veins, filled her with a simmering anticipation. It had been a long time since she'd been in a situation like this, a long time since she'd been with a man she truly desired. She thought— was fairly certain—that it had been a long time for Nate, as well, but he seemed to feel no urge to rush.

And yet…and yet, she could hear the shaky rush of his breathing, feel the rapid pounding of his heart beneath her palm, knew he was not unaffected by this heady excitement, that his control came at a cost. The knowledge sent a thrill racing along her nerve paths and she opened her mouth, allowing her tongue to seek pleasure within his. With a low moan, he countered her move, opening up a new and seductive vista in their mounting ardor. The embrace that had been tenderly controlled, gently leading, became firm, purposeful, demanding. His arms tightened around her, his lips bruised hers with his hunger and he gleaned the promise of passion from her mouth.

His hand moved to her waist then, negotiating with the hem of her sweater for entrance and proceeding unerringly, without hesitation or doubt, to cup the fullness of her breast in his palm. It was clear instantly he had experience in pleasuring, was practiced in the art of seduction, and understood the value and beauty of foreplay. His touch left her aching, needy. His kisses pledged sensual delights yet to come. His confidence assured her she was in very capable hands.

Miranda had thought making love with Nate would be satisfying, lovely, perhaps, but nothing out of the ordinary. He was, after all, a lot older than she and, somehow, in her planning, that had seemed a plus. She would be the seductress, he would be her willing slave. Or some similar scenario. Not for a second had she expected this…this rash, reckless feeling that she could not only surrender to the experience, but find pure delight in doing so. She, who never let herself feel out of control, felt suddenly, perfectly free to follow the roller-coaster ride of tension and release, the fast-slow escalation of desire, to leave the *how* of it in his obviously expert hands.

That wasn't like her. Not at all. But maybe there was some truth, after all, in the idea that the right man at the right time could change a woman's mind. About a lot of things.

He broke the kiss, abruptly, pulled back to look down at her with eyes darkened by longing. "Miranda," he said.

Just that. Her name. A husky question and answer, woven together. She knew the question, he knew the answer. This was simply a moment to savor the knowing, to anticipate, to wonder.

"Nathaniel," she whispered. Just that and nothing more.

He took her hand, enclosed it in the large warmth of his palm and led her toward the hallway. But only a few steps into the journey to the red satin sheets, he stopped, turned to give her a kiss that couldn't wait. Another step, and it was she who stopped him, wrapping her arms around his neck, drawing his head down to hers, prolonging the suspense, feeding the fire. When he pinned her to the wall, she knew it was justly deserved…and excessively satisfying. Hunger made ravenous by the anticipation. Desire slaked like a long thirst, only to return the instant his lips left hers. Passion increased a thousand times over with every sensual pause.

Neither his sweater nor hers made it as far as the bedroom door, having disappeared somewhere in the hall, sacrifices to his—and her—insatiable need to touch. Flesh to hands. Hands to flesh. Lips caressing.

Sighs intermingled. Behind them the light spilled into the hall. Before them, moonlight danced through an unshaded window. Between them, eagerness thrummed an overture they both knew and yet had never heard before.

They reached the bed eventually, losing shoes, socks, everything that hindered the desire to touch without limitations, to discover and explore each other. There was magic, then, within the small bedroom, as he guided her down onto the satin sheets. Cool, yes, beneath her...which felt lovely to her fevered skin. Slick, too, and sinfully inviting as Nate slid down beside her.

Miranda lost track of time after that, measured the moments in kisses, in the low throaty sounds of pleasure. His. And hers. She had never been a nonparticipant and met his every challenge with one of her own. She stroked him, nibbled him, caressed him and yet surrendered control again and again to the raw need his practiced touch so easily aroused. He was far and away the best lover she'd ever imagined, much less had, and he teased and titillated, soothed and satisfied, until she was weak with wanting and ready. So ready.

Then, and only then, did he fit his strength into the softness of her and begin a strangely new seduction. Their bodies found a pleasurable rhythm, which moved too quickly toward a climax. Nate slowed the movement, seduced her again with kisses, settled anew into harmonious agreement. All too soon, Miranda reached a crashing, breathtaking, glorious climax.

Breathing hard, yet hardly breathing, she gloried in the sweetness of kisses moist with their lovemaking, touches grown lazy in purpose, loving in repose. The afterglow cradled them, kept their bodies entwined, satisfied. For the moment.

"Mmm." He sighed as he propped his head on his hand, gazed lovingly down at her. "Thank God you plan ahead."

"I made a list," she confessed.

"You're a wanton woman, Miranda Danville. Devious, wildly sexy and determined to have your way with me." He kissed her, and her response was to slide her palm across his chest, tangling her fingers in the hair that curled there, teasing him with fingertips that were both wanton and determined. He captured her hand before it could move lower and she could have her way with him again. "I can't tell you how happy I am to have discovered your secret vices and I will be encouraging you to use them against me…very shortly."

She smiled, lazily, longingly. "Who knew," she whispered.

"Who knew what?" he asked.

That she could give herself over so completely to

a man. That he would be such a passionate lover. That the two of them would be so good together. But she voiced none of those thoughts, just offered him the parting of her lips in another invitation. "Who knew," she whispered, "that red satin sheets would be such an aphrodisiac."

Chapter Nine

"Miranda? We have a, uh, slight problem with the caterer."

Miranda had been doodling—*doodling!*—on her notepad, lost in a pleasant daydream about Nate. It had been nearly a month since the night at the beach house. One whole month of working on the coffee-house together, talking about plans for his mother's gardens, stealing time to spend together not talking at all. At least, not talking in the conventional way. Or maybe it was conventional. Maybe scheduling time alone between work commitments and children was a very conventional means of communication between a man and a woman. It certainly had added an air of clandestine excitement to their rendezvous. And the knowledge that interruptions were the norm rather than the exception made her appreciate the moments when alone with Nate.

Yet, she had discovered the truth in what she'd

told him, too. She loved the noisy minutes. The times when all four of his children were speaking at once about four different subjects at four different volumes. Those times with his children brought back memories of how she and her siblings had talked to and around one another, vying for attention, talking just to hear themselves talk, talking to see if anyone was listening.

Nate listened to his children. At least, he tried hard to do so. Often, she thought, he tried too hard. In his attempts to field their questions right and left, he missed the point more than half the time. He didn't seem to remember at times that Will and Cate were thirteen and wanted to be treated like adults, but still needed to know there were boundaries. He forgot sometimes that Kali and Kori simply needed a lot of reassurance. Miranda had just been thinking of ways she could help him up his batting average, when Ainsley walked into her office.

Giving up her distraction with some reluctance, Miranda smiled at her sister, remembering somewhat belatedly that in just a little more than a week, Baby would be married and a wife. How was that possible? And yet, Miranda was ready for the wedding of the year to be over. It seemed as if she had nothing else on her mind for weeks and weeks. But now that she actually thought about it, she realized with a start that since the night at the beach house—

no, since the day of the fire…or had it begun even before that?—she'd hardly given the wedding plans a thought. Which was not like her. Not in the least. Ordinarily, she'd have been on the phone, checking and double-checking to make sure everything was ready for the big event. Ordinarily, she'd have been a little stressed, but completely confident that all her careful planning was about to pay off. Ordinarily, she wouldn't have been spending even five seconds of her day doodling—*doodling!*—and daydreaming. Pulling herself up short, she made a mental promise to give this entire week to Ainsley and not let anything or anyone—Nate, in particular—distract her.

"What sort of problem?" she asked, sounding calm, amazed after a quick internal check to realize she *was* calm. "Are they going to have trouble getting the lobster, after all?"

"Mmm, yes and no." Ainsley stood on the opposite side of the desk, lacing her fingers into an uncertain knot, rocking slightly back and forth on her heels. "But mainly, no. I mean, yes, no lobster."

Miranda maintained her smile, knowing the dam would break in a minute and Ainsley would blurt out the problem. With its accompanying explanation. Ainsley always had an explanation.

"Maybe I'll sit down," Ainsley said, although she continued to stand.

It struck Miranda suddenly, irrelevantly, that she

rarely saw any one of her siblings at her office unless they needed help. She was in Matt's office at the Foundation almost daily for one reason or another, but he only came to her when trouble was brewing over a fund-raiser or among the volunteers and staff. Andrew often dropped by to get her opinion about set designs or which of several photos she liked best, but seldom, if ever, just to talk. Ainsley, well, she usually blew in and out in a matter of ten or fifteen minutes, leaving whatever problem she'd brought with her in Miranda's capable hands.

Usually, Miranda waited for the delivery, but today she was too impatient. "So, we need to choose another entrée?" Miranda asked impatiently.

"Something like that," Ainsley answered.

"Then we'll choose a different entrée. I'll call the caterer right now and straighten this out." She didn't quite understand why Ainsley hadn't done that herself. It wasn't that difficult, after all. But maybe this was her way of getting Miranda's attention. Reaching for the phone, Miranda looked expectantly at her sister. "Do you have the phone number with you?"

Ainsley shook her head.

Miranda offered a slight smile, not truly surprised or dismayed by the information. Phone numbers for the various wedding contractors—all of them, with notes—were in a notebook in the middle-right-hand drawer of her desk. But she didn't automatically reach for them. This was Ainsley's wedding. It would be good for her to feel a little of the burden of planning it…even though it was a little late in the game for that.

"The problem with the caterer," Ainsley explained, sinking finally into the chair, managing to barely sit on the edge of it, "is that we don't, exactly, have one."

Panic slid down Miranda's spine and she had the drawer open and her own wedding notebook on the desktop in a flash. "Of course we have a caterer," she said. "We hired Katherine Claiborne's firm two months ago. Remember? I made the preliminary contact. We went together and talked to Katherine in person, and then you and Ivan followed up with an appointment to sign the contract." But Ainsley had forgotten to make that appointment. Miranda inhaled a deep breath, hoping to bring patience in along with it. "You didn't follow up with Katherine."

It wasn't a question, and she didn't even need to see the look on Ainsley's face to confirm this. "I meant to, Miranda, honestly. I even actually thought I'd taken care of it, but somehow, well, the contract just got overlooked."

Overlooked. Because Ainsley had *expected* someone else to handle the details. Because she was *ac-*

customed to having someone else handle the details. Because, based on past experience, she knew someone else *would* handle the details. And Miranda had always encouraged her to believe that someone else *would* do it. And there it was, in a nutshell. Ainsley hadn't followed through with the caterer because she had expected Miranda to remind her. That was their pattern. Ainsley dawdled, Miranda prodded, and eventually the little detail was handled. Occasionally by Ainsley. Most of the time by Miranda.

Except this time Miranda had allowed someone else to distract her…and the detail had now become a problem.

"I'm sorry, Miranda. Really. I know there's no excuse for it, and Ivan's been helping me this morning, trying to locate someone else. Only we haven't had much luck. I realize it's late notice and all, but I thought we'd be able to find someone. The Danville Foundation uses a lot of catering services and I know you like to spread the events around, so I was sure at least one of the caterers I called would recognize my name and try to accommodate us, but I seem to have left it a little late even for a Danville." Her chin dipped for a moment and she pressed her lips together…a sign, Miranda had learned, that usually meant there was still more to the story. "Except…Ivan did find one caterer who could handle the reception."

It was her tone of voice, more than anything else, that made Miranda's heart sink. "Well," she said, hoping she was wrong. "Fortunately, one is all we need."

"You might not think so when I tell you who it is."

Worst fear confirmed, Miranda thought with a sigh. "It's Julian Morris, the caterer who ruined Scott's wedding."

"How did you know that?"

"Murphy's Law."

"He's the only one we've found who'd even talk to us," Ainsley said in self-defense.

"And there's a reason for that, Ainsley. Think about it."

Ainsley sighed. "I'll cancel if you can think of a better option."

"A better option?" Miranda was angry suddenly. At Ainsley for leaving something so important to the last minute. At herself for attempting to delegate some of the responsibility to the bride—who had said she was grown up. At their mother for not being here, for never being here. "If you and I did all the food preparation ourselves, it would be a better option than using Julian Morris. He doesn't have a clue how to cater a big event. Honestly, Ainsley, how could you let this happen? Do you want your wedding to be a complete disaster?"

Tears pooled in the blue eyes staring back at her, and though Ainsley tried hard to blink them away, they had the desired effect. Miranda softened. As she always did. She accepted her share of the blame. As she always did. She began to think of how best to fix the problem. As she always did.

"I'll call Katherine," she said. "She'll talk to me. That's no guarantee she'll take on your reception at the absolute last minute, but I'll do what I can."

Ainsley leaned forward and picked up a river rock, worn silky smooth by the tumbling water of the Amazon. It had been brought home by their parents from some long-ago mission trip and used ever since by Miranda as a paperweight. She had always considered it an appropriate symbol of her role in the family. The rock. The one who held firm while the others' lives flowed over and around her.

"Oh, don't be modest, Miranda. You'll manage to convince her she's been waiting for your call and that catering my wedding reception at the last minute is the opportunity she's been waiting for all her life."

"Don't count on it. There's a good chance she has other commitments and simply can't do it. It was probably iffy two months ago when I first called her, but now…"

"But now, I've made it impossible." Ainsley

turned the rock in her hand, then returned it abruptly to the desk. "I did say I was sorry."

"Yes, you did. Maybe it's my turn to apologize to you."

Ainsley looked up. "For what?"

"I haven't been…myself lately."

"You haven't?" She seemed genuinely surprised by the thought and a little amused. "Who have you been?"

"Very funny. But you know as well as I do that I've been somewhat preoccupied for the past few weeks and I do intend to make it up to you, Baby. I will."

Dual creases formed a cute little frown between Ainsley's eyebrows. Now that she'd confessed her sin of omission and been absolved of responsibility, her bouncy good humor had returned like the sunlight after a summer shower. "Goody," she said. "I know just how you can do it, too."

It was Miranda's turn to frown…except not so cutely. "I was thinking we'd spend a lot of time together this week, making sure no other neglected details turn into problems."

"And I was thinking you'd tell me all about you and Nate, right here, right now."

Miranda should have expected that. "Nothing to tell," she replied blithely. "Except that the coffeehouse is coming along nicely and will open next

Friday, as planned. It's turned out to be a very…
interesting project.''

"I wouldn't call Nate Shepard a *project*.''

"His coffeehouse, on the other hand, clearly is.''

Ainsley sat back in her chair, smiling like the
Cheshire cat. "Come on, Miranda. Give me details.
I want all the romantic details.''

"It would be more beneficial if we talked about
your wedding, instead. And more interesting.''

"No, it wouldn't. I don't care about the wedding,
Miranda. Well, of course, I do care, but only about
the marrying-Ivan part, not about the rest of it. I care
about you. I'm your sister. And a matchmaker. You
can talk to me. I mean, I know what's going on,
anyway.''

"You don't know what's happening with your
own wedding, Ainsley. So I doubt very seriously
you have a clue as to what's actually happening in
my life.''

Ainsley's smile faded and Miranda felt badly for
snapping at her. But for her to sit there and say she
didn't care about the wedding was too much. Especially after all the work they'd already put into it.
And wanting to talk about Nate, which Miranda had
no intention of doing, was just simple avoidance.
Another way to ignore the details that needed at-
tending to. Nate was fun. She liked being with him.

Maybe a little more than she'd planned, but that was neither here nor there. And did not merit discussion.

"You might be surprised to discover I do have a clue," Ainsley said, sitting forward as her expression turned serious. "Contrary to your apparent belief that I wander through life totally self-absorbed, I actually do care what happens to you and want you to find that special someone to share your life. I think maybe Nate is that someone. But I'm only guessing, of course. Because you never share the details of your life. Not with me. Not with Matt. Not with Andrew. You just go off and fall in love without a word to your brothers or your sister. The three people who would genuinely like to share some part in your happiness."

"There is nothing to share, Ainsley. I didn't go off and…and fall in love, as you put it. I'd tell you if my…friendship…with Nate was something lasting, but it's not. It's just a…"

"A fling?" Ainsley offered. "You don't have flings, Miranda. You don't have affairs. You barely even bother to date anymore. Suddenly, Nate comes along and you're different. You're wearing a secret little smile, you're distracted, you forget to remind me to call the caterer. I think that's great. You deserve to be happy. You deserve a man like Nate. I just wish you didn't feel you have to hide what's happening from me. I'm your sister. I'm happy for you.''

''That's nice, but—''

''Don't treat me like a child, Miranda. I can see for myself that you're in love with him, whether you'll admit it or not. I know his children adore you already. I can totally see you running their lives as efficiently and lovingly as you've always run ours. But I'd love to hear all that from you. The details of how you feel, how excited you are, how scared you are at times. I'd love to listen to you ramble on about him the way I ramble on about Ivan. I'd like to think my opinion mattered to you. I do have one, you know. I'm a matchmaker, Miranda, and I'm good at it. I just wish you could see that and let me help you sometimes instead of feeling as if your only role in my life is to rescue me every time I make a mistake.''

Miranda was shaking inside, sifting through the torrent of words for the few that had knotted in her stomach. ''I'm not in love with Nate Shepard,'' she said firmly, feeling it was important to be clear on that point first. ''And I certainly have no intention of running his life or the lives of his children.'' Another thought—one that had occurred to her before but that came back stronger this time. ''Did you do this, Ainsley? Did you set up this...this *match* for me?''

For once, Ainsley didn't make any attempt to explain. She got to her feet and stood, her usual saucy attitude concealed behind a look that seemed almost…mature. There was a sparkle of possibilities in her eyes, a new confidence in the arch of her eyebrows. "I've got to go back to work," she said evenly. "As hard as it may be to believe, I actually have clients who pay me to help them find love. Not everyone, Miranda, stumbles blindly into the best thing that ever happened to them."

Miranda had a pithy answer for that. She knew she did. She just couldn't remember it at the moment, and so Ainsley walked out of her office unchallenged.

For a long time afterward, Miranda sat there, frowning, trying to make sense of it, trying to decipher fact from fiction. Ainsley had an active imagination. She always had. That's all this was. A combination of imagination and prewedding jitters. She was getting married and she felt scared of leaving home, afraid that Miranda would no longer be there to handle the details of her life anymore. That's what this was about. Anxiety over leaving the security of home. Trying to put Miranda on the defensive was just a ploy—probably an unconscious one—an attempt to worry about something other than the major step into adulthood she was about to make. That's what this was about.

And Ainsley had a right to be upset. For over a month now—and if she were truthful, she'd admit it had been since the first day she'd walked into the coffeehouse—Miranda had neglected her real life in favor of a fantasy life. She'd abandoned responsibility...as her parents had done throughout her life. Except that they had a legitimate reason, a higher calling.

Miranda didn't. She'd chosen a long time ago, even before she was old enough to make such a choice, to take on the role of designated parent. Someone needed to do it and so she had. And now that her role was changing, maybe she felt a little scared herself. But that was no reason to rush out and find another family whose lives she could, as Ainsley had put it, *totally run.* She didn't want that. She wanted to be free. She wanted to know what that felt like. She didn't want the responsibility of other lives. She didn't.

And she wasn't in love. She would have known. This...these feelings she had were simply the afterglow of a strong physical attraction, an outgrowth of Nate's easy companionship. She didn't want to be in love with him. So therefore, she wasn't. She was in control of her emotions. And she meant to keep it that way.

She'd had a plan going into this. Now she'd simply have to make a plan to end it.

Right after she called Katherine, the caterer, and begged for a reprieve.

It wasn't what she wanted to do, but it had to be done. Someone had to be the rock.

"DAD!" Kali, red plaid ribbons flying, raced to the back room of the coffeehouse, where Nate was putting storage shelves together.

"Dad!" Kori, red-and-white polka-dot ribbons bouncing against her dark hair, was barely a step behind. "The truck is here."

"The truck is here!" Kali repeated. "With the furniture! Call Miranda! Quick! Tell her to get here fast!"

Nate laid aside his electric screwdriver and got to his feet, grinning at the girls' excitement. A few weeks ago, they'd wanted nothing to do with the coffeehouse. But that had been before Miranda suggested they set up a play area for the children who would accompany their parents out for a cappuccino. He owed her big-time for that idea. "What do we need Miranda for?" he teased. "She's not going to unload the furniture. The men in the truck will do that."

Kori slipped a fisted hand to her waist, which reminded Nate of the way Angie used to show mock impatience. Kali rolled her expressive eyes, also resembling her mother. "Miranda has to tell you where to put the stuff, Dad," she said.

"That's right, Dad," Kori echoed. "How else will we know where it goes?"

"Maybe I know where it goes. Ever thought of that?"

Their foreheads creased in identical frowns. "No," they answered in unison as they grabbed his hand—one apiece—and tugged him out of the storeroom. "Come on, Dad. Call her. Call her now."

It was amazing, when he thought about it, how quickly Miranda had become a part of his life. The Kays were completely enamored of her and were constantly thinking of things to ask her, making plans that included her. Will and Cate behaved more cautiously, but then they were more interested in themselves at any given moment than in what their dad had going on.

And what he had going on was special. He knew that, even if they didn't. He didn't mind sharing…a little…but he had no intention of making his courtship a family project.

Kali and Kori stopped tugging on his hands and gave him identical stern looks. "Call her, Dad."

He would have, gladly. Except that he'd already phoned Miranda once today and he'd been able to tell by her voice that she was under stress. The details of Ainsley's wedding, probably, accounted for the cool tone. He wished he could do something to help, wished mostly that she'd let him help. But Miranda hadn't quite grasped the idea of sharing responsibility yet. That might take some time.

And still the twins were waiting for him to make the call.

"Miranda said she'd come to the coffeehouse as soon as she finishes with the landscape crew. I'm sure she'll be here any minute." He put a hand at their backs and herded them toward the front door. "In the meantime, you two watch from over here while I supervise the unloading."

But Miranda still hadn't arrived an hour later when the chaise longues sat, wrapped in plastic, and the black-and-white-tiled bar had been securely situated inside the outline Miranda had taped out on the floor. She was so precise about things like that. Plan your work, work your plan. That was her motto. More like a creed, really. He loved that about her. But then he loved just about everything about her. No point in denying it. He was smitten. Truly, deeply. He knew it to be true every time he saw her or heard her voice or simply thought about her. Which he did a lot.

He hadn't expected to fall in love again. Angie had assured him he would. She'd told him she was in favor of it. She'd made him swear he wouldn't let a misguided sense of loyalty to her memory keep him from claiming happiness whenever it found him. Life, she had often reminded him, was too short to spend in regrets. He realized now what a gift she had given him by offering her blessing long before he'd had any reason to believe he'd ever want it. Angie had always had amazing foresight. For all he knew, she could have orchestrated his first encounter with Miranda, pulled some heavenly strings to make sure the right woman caught his attention.

More and more, he was sure that Miranda *was* the right woman. He realized she wasn't convinced he was the right man, but it was early days yet. And he was a patient man. Older, too, and willing to let her discover in her own sweet time that she was in love with him. Experience had taught him that some things were worth the wait.

He just hoped it would happen soon.

MIRANDA HAD HER PLAN firmly in mind when she walked into the coffeehouse. She was late. Over an hour late and hadn't a single excuse to offer. Except that she had dreaded this moment all day and put it off as long as she could.

"Miranda! Miranda!" Her name doubled as the twins barreled across the room to greet her with a low-slung hug. "Wait'll you see the new furniture. Wait'll you see what we've done."

They were like duplicate tornadoes, little funnels

of energy and excitement, flinging themselves into the moment with pure abandon, welcoming her into their day without reservation, whether she wanted to be there or not. They reminded her of Ainsley and Andrew at a similar age. Except that she had been too young then to appreciate the special set of warm feelings that came with being important to a pair of seven-year-olds. She wondered how long they would miss her after today and hated that she had ever let herself grow attached to them. Or them to her. She didn't want children. She didn't want to be the designated parent to another set of twins. And Nate had two sets. Four children who wanted a mother. Even a poor facsimile of one.

Better to make the ending swift and pain them all as little as possible.

"Miranda."

Nate's voice flowed over her like a beloved song, offering his welcome in the sound of her name and a husky pleasure that promised a more intimate greeting offstage. She steeled herself to look at him, telling herself she was not in love with him. Not yet. Not immune to the possibility, maybe, but not there yet, either. She still had time to walk away unscathed. Free and clear.

"We thought you'd never get here," he said and his smile changed her opinion. Not free. Not entirely. "The girls have been dying to know where

you want the chaise longues. They're especially
fond of the red one. I'm rather partial to the yellow.''

She cleared her throat. ''I...we need to talk,'' she
replied quickly, before she lost her nerve. ''Alone.''

A frown creased his forehead and vanished into a
smile. ''The most frightening words a man ever
hears from a woman are *we need to talk.* Did you
know that?''

She shook her head, telling herself she could get
through this if he just didn't touch her.

''Well, it's true,'' he continued. ''On the other
hand, I like that *alone* part you've added.''

She had to do this. No matter how much the
thought of it made her sick at heart. ''Nate, I...look,
this isn't easy for me, but I know it's the right decision.''

His smile began to fade. ''This sounds serious.
Maybe you should hold on to those words until we
are alone.''

''Miranda! Look at us! We made a tent!''

Across the room, the twins had crawled under one
of the chaise longues, using the plastic as a tent.
They wanted her attention and would be back in an
instant to claim it. Now was not the time for serious
discussion. Except...there was nothing to discuss.
''I'm not going to see you anymore,'' she said
evenly, wondering how she could sound so certain

when her whole body trembled, when it felt as if the world was spinning down around her.

His eyes held hers…gravity in the midst of chaos. "Now you're scaring me," he said, his hand reaching up to brush her cheek, sending a familiar longing thrilling through her and denying in a gesture what she'd spent all day convincing herself was true. She couldn't do this, couldn't not do it. But it had to be now. She had to convince him now. Before the poignant touch of his hand persuaded her she was making an awful mistake.

"I'm sorry," she whispered. "I can't see you anymore."

His other hand came up to settle persuasively, firmly, on her shoulder. "It isn't that easy, Miranda. I won't let it be that easy."

"Miranda!" The twins yelled again. Outside, a horn honked. Then another. A bell jangled. The door opened. The clutter of the outside world swept in. Somehow she managed to keep breathing.

"Hey, what does a fellow have to do to get a cup of coffee in this town?"

The voice was familiar, deep and resonant, and went through Miranda like a memory she couldn't quite place.

"Uncle Nicky! Uncle Nicky!"

The girls were out of their tent and throwing themselves into the embrace of a tall, spectacularly handsome man. Nick Shepard. Nate's brother. The first man—boy—Miranda had fallen in love with. She had been crazy about him once, briefly. Who would have thought she'd be so happy to see him now? If only for the interruption he caused, the respite he provided. She turned from Nate to Nick with a good deal more enthusiasm than she felt.

"Nick," she said, forcing a false vibrancy into her voice. "Nick Shepard."

He stopped hugging his nieces and focused his dark, matinee-idol eyes on her, his smile shifting smoothly into a practiced and perfected charisma. "Miranda?" he said, rising slowly to his feet. "Miranda Danville?"

She managed a nod, which he seemed to take as shyness, because his smile shifted again, became coaxing, cajoling. A smile she imagined his soap-opera fans knew very well. "Now this," he said in a voice meant only for her, "is what I call a welcome-home party." He came forward, never taking his eyes off her, making her the focus of his whole attention. "Hello, Miranda." And he leaned in to kiss her on the cheek, as if they were old and dear friends, separated only by the time it took to reestablish their history. His lips butterfly-brushed her skin, a move both friendly and seductive. All within the span of a heartbeat. He stepped back, still smiling down at her and, somehow—she didn't know how he'd accomplished it—he was holding her hands...both hands, clasped warmly, firmly, in the cradle of his palms. "Hi, Nate," he said casually, but his eyes still held Miranda's.

"Nick," Nate responded. "What a surprise."

Not an especially pleasant one, it seemed to Miranda. But then, that could be the circumstances. In Nate's view, this could hardly be a welcome interruption.

"Had a few days off. Thought I'd drive up to check out this coffeehouse deal I've been hearing about and hang around for the grand opening this weekend." He surveyed the room, letting Miranda's hands go free a second before she would have freed them herself. "Your taste has improved, bro," Nick said. "This place actually looks trendy. You may be on to something here."

"Uncle Nicky, come see our tent." Kori pulled on her uncle's hand.

Kali tugged on the other. "Come see the toys Miranda bought."

"In a minute, kiddos." His smile kept them all within his orbit, even when he spoke to Nate. "Where's my nephew? Is he as tall as I am yet? And the lovely Cate...where is she?"

"They're still at school. Cate's in drama. Will's at wrestling practice. I'll pick them up in—" Nate checked his watch ''—about thirty minutes. Are you staying at the house?''

Nick's laughter was deep, rich, full of nuance...and Miranda knew he was giving her a sample of countless years of voice lessons. ''Where else would I go?'' he said with another on-camera smile. ''Home is where the heart is, you know.''

''Great.'' Nate slipped a hand against the small of her back. ''Miranda and I are going across the street for a cup of coffee. Entertain your nieces for a few minutes.''

Miranda panicked. She didn't want to talk. She wanted to escape now before he convinced her they had a future. All of them. Him and his two sets of twins. ''I can't,'' she said, moving pointedly away from his touch. ''I have an appointment. About the wedding.'' She turned to Nick, pretending she had no hidden agenda. ''My baby sister is getting married. A week from Saturday. Maybe you'll stay in town long enough to come to the wedding.''

He misread the invitation. She saw it in the interest that flashed in his eyes, the hint of satisfaction that crept into his smile. It all came back to her— the ease with which he'd charmed her teenage self, the way he'd played her emotions, kept her unsure and adoring. She realized now he'd been a good actor then. But he was a whole lot better now. ''I would love to come,'' he replied. ''Love to. Where's your appointment? I need to pick up a few things at the store before I go up to the house. Can I give you a lift? I've got the Aston.''

As if she would be impressed by a sports car.

''Take me! Take me!'' Kali hopped up and down with eagerness.

''Me, too, Uncle Nicky! Me, too!''

''Girls,'' Nate said sternly, and they subsided. ''Miranda,'' he said, ''I think we need a few minutes alone. To talk.''

Nick laughed. ''You're sounding mysterious, brother. Not to mention a little serious. Although I'll admit to a healthy curiosity about finding you here in my brother's new business venture, Miranda.''

''Miranda and I are—''

''I'm the decorator.'' Miranda cut off Nate's explanation, drawing Nick's attention easily. ''I've been helping your brother get this place ready for the opening on Saturday. But my part is done. Nothing left to do but set the furniture in place and brew the coffee.'' She thought her voice sounded a pitch too high, her delivery a tad too fast, but it was the best she could do. ''And now, I really must leave.''

''Let me give you a lift,'' Nick repeated, upping the charm in his ready smile, ignoring, or not even noticing, the tension rocketing from Nate to her and back again. ''Anywhere you want to go.''

At one time, his offer would have made her go

weak at the knees with delight. Similar to the twins'
reaction. But now, all she could think about was
how to get away from Nate's questioning gaze, how
to avoid having him come after her and demand an
explanation she didn't want to give.

And there was a way. Right in front of her. Nick.
If she'd been destined to fall in love with one of the
Shepard brothers, why couldn't she have done it in
reverse order? Why couldn't she have had a heart-
breaking crush on Nate all those years ago and a
casual affair with Nick all these years later? That
would have made more sense, really. Nick was the
brother she should be with now. He was the free
spirit, the one who did as he pleased, with never a
hint of responsibility to anyone but himself. That
was the life she wanted now that she no longer
needed to fill the role of surrogate parent.

Wasn't it?

"I'd appreciate a ride, Nick," she said, surprising
herself as well as Nate, who looked at her as if she'd
lost her mind.

And maybe she had. But in the long run, she figured that was better than losing her heart.

"But…" She checked her watch, not even registering the time. "I have to go now or I'll be late
for my appointment."

"I am at your disposal." Nick took her arm, es-
corting her to the door, tossing Nate and his nieces

an over-the-shoulder goodbye. "I'll see you guys later at the house." His grin was easy, his tone teasing. "Kali, Kori, you two will never guess what I've brought you this time. Be ready for a big surprise."

That was enough to set the twins off again, hopping about and making silly guesses in their squeaky little-girl voices.

As she and Nick stepped outside into the waning daylight, Miranda listened for Nate's voice, calming the girls, calling her back.

But, as best she could tell, he didn't say a single word.

Chapter Ten

Lucinda opened the door of Ainsley's office and stepped back to let the four Shepard children file in. Then, with an I-have-no-idea shrug directed at Ainsley, she closed the door and left matchmaker and clients alone.

"Hello." Ainsley pushed up from her chair as the children formed a solemn line in front of her desk, the identical twins in the middle, alike in the blue jumpers and white blouses that formed their school uniforms, different only in the design of the ribbons that adorned their hair. On either side, like a set of bookends, the older twins stood, also in navy and white—Cate in a navy pleated skirt, Will in navy slacks, as different as twins could be, but wearing the same troubled expression.

"I know we should have called first," Cate said. "But we had to see you. Something's happened."

Ainsley was well aware of it. Something had happened. But she didn't know if her perspective and that of Nate's children would be the same. There was, after all, bad and not so bad. It depended on which side of the *something* a person stood. "Sit." She gestured at the chairs behind them, and the little girls promptly took a seat, their thin legs extending awkwardly from the edge of the chair. Will hesitated, waiting maybe for Cate to sit down. But when she didn't, he, too, remained standing.

Ainsley sank into her chair again and picked up a pen. Not that she expected to take notes, but the weight of the ballpoint in her hand helped remind her at times that she was a professional. "Tell me," she said, inviting confidence…which came at her all at once, in four different voices, four different volumes, four different versions.

"It's Dad…"

"Miranda and Uncle Nicky…"

"She didn't look at our tent and…"

"Uncle Nicky forgot all about our surprise, too!"

It was four tales of grievance, children trying to make sense of the adults in their lives, talking because they needed someone to hear them. Ainsley discovered a lovely satisfaction in just listening and she wondered if her parents had felt anything like this when she and Andrew, Matt and Miranda were young and vying to be heard. Except, a lot of the time, most of the time, really, it had been only Miranda listening, only Miranda trying to sort out what was true and what was not.

"We think Dad is mad at Uncle Nick."

"Miranda didn't even tell us where to put the red chase."

"Uncle Nicky said he'd take us to the movie and now he won't!"

"'Cause he's always with Miranda."

Ainsley let them talk it out, gleaning facts she already knew and a couple she didn't. Everything had been fine—in the Shepard children's eyes, at least—until their uncle showed up. Then suddenly, Miranda had abandoned them and was spending time with Nick and not with them. Not only was their dad mad about it, they were mad, too. It wasn't fair and everything had been going along so well until *bam!* It all fell apart.

That wasn't what they said, exactly, but it was what they were feeling. That much Ainsley knew. What she didn't know was what exactly had happened to cause her practical, levelheaded sister to drop a promising relationship with one brother to take up with the other. Not that Ainsley thought for a second Miranda was involved with Nick Shepard. Miranda wasn't impressed with good looks—although, admittedly, Nick had that in spades—and she certainly didn't have any secret fascination with fame—Nick had that, as well. He'd been Miranda's first brush with love, the first boy to kiss her, the closest encounter she'd ever had with not being in complete charge of her emotions. Until Nate came along, a stronger, better version of his brother, in Ainsley's humble opinion, Miranda hadn't gotten within ten yards of a man who posed any danger to her heart.

Ainsley had known when Miranda arrived at Danfair the evening before last in Nick's flashy sports car and then rushed out with him again a little later on the pretext of retrieving her Mercedes, which she'd left at her office for some unknown reason, that something had happened between her and Nate. Miranda didn't do things on the spur of the moment like that, for one thing. And for another, it didn't take until midnight to retrieve a car parked less than five miles away. Ainsley's sisterly antennae had gone up, but her matchmaker instincts had advised her this sudden departure from the norm was a good sign.

It meant, in Ainsley's professional opinion, that Miranda was running scared and making an all-out effort to convince herself and anyone watching that she was not in love with Nate. But until this moment, Ainsley hadn't understood why. Four reasons stared her in the face, bombarding her with words, representing the past Miranda was so afraid of repeating.

These four children were not so dissimilar from
the children she, Miranda, Andrew and Matt had
once been. The Shepard children needed a mother,
someone to look to for guidance, comfort, love…all
the things Miranda had given so selflessly to her
siblings over the years. Ainsley understood suddenly
that Miranda had been afraid all those years, afraid
that one of them—or all of them—would need
something more than she could provide.

Ainsley's heart ached then for the responsibility
Miranda had borne so willingly, swelled with love
for all her sister had given her without her ever realizing what it had cost.

But that was the past. There was one important
difference in the present. The Shepard children already had someone to guide them, comfort and love
them. They had Nate. And loving Nate—and as a
bonus, his children—was all anyone expected from
Miranda.

Ainsley felt as if she'd just solved a complicated
puzzle.

"…and I don't like this."

"Dad needs Miranda to tell him where the furniture goes."

"I want her to be with us, not Uncle Nicky."

"We have to do something."

They wrapped up their translation of events in a
staggered ending, each voice trailing away in con-

fusion, each gaze finding its way across the desk again. "We have to do something," Cate repeated, pulling all of their frustration into a single plea for help. "Anything. We just want Dad to be happy again."

Ainsley wasn't entirely sure Nathaniel Shepard would welcome their help. She was certain Miranda wouldn't.

But then, Nate and Miranda weren't her clients. These four children were.

"I'll think of something," she promised rashly. "Don't worry. That's my job. I'm good at it and I *will* think of something."

NICK SHEPARD WAS everything Miranda had ever thought she wanted in a man.

He made plans sporadically and changed them on a whim. He lived on the edge and loved it. He answered to no one but himself, took pleasure where he found it and made no apology for it. Life was big and he was living it.

It took less than twenty-four hours for his *joie de vivre* to drive Miranda crazy.

She didn't know how anyone could live at such a pace. She didn't understand, nor much appreciate, his style of spontaneity. She didn't care if his glamorous lifestyle wasn't...as he put it...all it was cracked up to be. She only knew she couldn't live that way. She needed routine, schedules, plans. She needed stability and steadiness. She needed...Nate.

She longed for him with a frightening intensity, missed him as if he'd been out of her life for months instead of hours. And, although she told herself freedom was what she wanted, in the early-morning dusk of a new day, she acknowledged that she might have made an awful mistake.

THE COFFEEHOUSE SPORTED signage in scripted lights with a steaming coffee cup at a tilt and the name A New Brew in bold colors beneath. The aroma of good coffee wafted out into the street every time someone opened the door. Inside could be heard the uneven rhythms of a fledgling band, good, but not quite star material yet, the laughter of children in the play area, the perking percolators, the bell jangling when anyone came in or out and the hum of conversations competing with the sizzling hiss of the cappuccino machine.

The grand opening was upon them and going great guns. Behind the black-and-white-tiled counter, Nate was tending bar, supervising his trainees and feeling all around pleased with the turnout. Only one thing—one person—was missing in this scenario he'd imagined a hundred times: Miranda.

And if she walked in the door right now with Nick, he'd be extremely happy to see her...and extremely tempted to punch his brother in the nose. Of course, he wouldn't. For one thing, Nick was liable to punch back. And for another, Nick was blissfully unaware he was doing anything wrong. Which was Nate's fault. He should have told Nicky straight out he loved Miranda and asked his brother to back off. Which Nicky would have done. Nick was often self-absorbed, but he wasn't unfeeling.

However, Nate had kept his own counsel, had mulled over Miranda's announcement that she couldn't see him anymore, and concluded she needed time to think about what that meant before he set about changing her mind. And he figured Nick could do more good than harm in that regard. There had never been much in the way of competition between he and his brother. If they'd been closer in age, Nate knew it would have been a different story. But as he was a dozen years older, that particular problem had never come up. Until now, when Miranda seemed to be trying to replace one brother with another.

He didn't like the feeling at all and knew it was simply an indicator that his feelings for Miranda had gone way past the point where he could let her go without a fight. And, in truth, if she hadn't let herself be pulled into Nicky's fantasyland of a life, Nate would have been worried sick. As it stood, he knew Miranda and he knew Nick and he was ninety-eight percent certain the two of them would run into a personality conflict sooner rather than later.

On the other hand, if Miranda had coolly walked out the door and back into her old routine, that—in Nate's view—would have signaled she had no doubts about what she'd said and that not seeing him again didn't represent a scary prospect.

He hoped she felt scared. He hoped she had second thoughts...lots of them. But most of all, he hoped she would walk through the door of the coffeehouse right then. He wanted to share this day with her. He wanted to share the rest of his life with her. And, patient man that he was, he was very impatient for the rest of his life to start.

He still had his eye on the door when, halfway through its frothing cycle, the cappuccino machine exploded.

"WHAT DO YOU MEAN you're not going?"

Miranda knew from the edgy tone in Ainsley's voice that not going to the grand opening of the coffeehouse was the right decision. It was obvious to her, even from her lolling position on the East Salon sofa, that the matchmaker had a plan, a *reintroduction of possibilities,* and Miranda had no intention of falling for it. "I'm not going," she repeated. "That's what I mean and that's what I'm doing—*not going.* But I hope you have a fabulous time. You can tell me all about it later if you want. Or not.'' She flipped a page in the magazine she had open on her lap, pretending she was interested in a lipstick ad, pretending not to notice Ainsley's agitation. It served her right, Miranda thought. She wasn't supposed to matchmake family members, anyway. She'd promised she wouldn't.

''Fine,'' Ainsley said finally. ''But you can't avoid Nate forever, you know. He's going to win his ward and he'll be sitting right next to you at the city council meetings. And you'll have to work with the landscapers at his house all through next spring. And…and sooner or later, you're going to want a cup of coffee.''

Miranda found herself smiling at that. Only a trace of a smile, but still… ''I'm giving up coffee,'' she replied reasonably.

''You're giving up a lot more than that,'' Ainsley announced, her voice full of doom and gloom. ''But what do I know? I'm just the baby of the family. I'm just an apprentice matchmaker. What could I possibly know about love?''

Miranda turned another page of the magazine. A little more forcefully than she intended. ''I know you wanted this thing with Nate to work out for me, Ains. I know you had the best of intentions. But not every story has a happy ending.''

''And just how do you see *your* story ending, Miranda? Because I have to tell you that from my standpoint, it doesn't look happy. Not happy at all." She turned and flounced from the room, leaving the words hovering in her wake.

But Miranda kept flipping pages, pretending she couldn't hear those words echoing in her heart.

Sometime later, halfway through another magazine, she heard the door chimes and the scuffling sound of Benito, the newest addition to a long list of household help, as he hurried to answer the door. There was a murmur of voices—Benito's halting English and a deep baritone that resonated with a familiar huskiness. *Emergency,* she heard, and was on her feet, around the billiards table and in the doorway before he came up the shallow stairs of the foyer and she saw him.

"Nate," she said, afraid something terrible had happened to one of the children, afraid they had needed her while she was blindly flipping pages in a stupid magazine. He looked sober and somber, the bearer of bad news, with his hair disheveled and one hand clenched at the unzipped opening of his jacket. "What's wrong? Is it one of the Kays?"

"No," he said. "The cappuccino machine malfunctioned. It blew up."

"My God, was anybody hurt?"

"No, but look...." He let go of the jacket and it fell open to reveal a white shirt streaked with a muddy stain. "I don't know if it can be saved, but I knew you'd give it your best shot."

She looked at the stain, raised a doubtful gaze to his. "You came all the way to Danfair and scared me half to death because of a *coffee stain?*"

His shrug wasn't sheepish in the least, as it should have been. "I just didn't think club soda would cut it this time."

"You're right, it won't and neither will your excuse."

"You're not worried about my shirt?"

"No, and I don't believe you are, either."

"Oh, I am. I'm very worried." He came a step closer.

She took a step back, fighting the impulse to fly into his arms and never leave. "What…what about the coffeehouse? The grand opening?"

"It's grand," he said as he took another step. And another. "You should be there. I kept watching for you, waiting. But you didn't come."

She opened her mouth to offer an excuse. Or a reason. But only a raspy whisper emerged from her throat. "No, I didn't. Who…who's making coffee now?"

"Nicky is minding the store." Nate smiled meaningfully. "He owes me a favor. Or two."

"Oh."

He stopped directly in front of her and she had to

make an effort to catch her breath. "And you, Miranda, owe me something, as well."

She inhaled and gathered her composure. "All right," she said. "You want an explanation, I'll give you one. Responsibility. I've had it all my life, Nate. I practically raised my brothers and sister. I...I can't do that again."

"That's good, because they're grown up. Have been, as best I can tell, for a long time now."

"Yes, but your children are still...well, children."

"Yes." He drew out the word, questioning, still not connecting the dots.

"They need a mother."

His gaze locked on hers, held fast. "Is that what this has all been about, Miranda? You think I want you in my life so my kids will have a mother?"

"No," she whispered. "Not exactly."

"Then what? Do you think I fell in love with you because you handle responsibility well?"

"No, but..."

"But nothing, Miranda. You know me better than that. I may not be the best father in the world, but I'm learning. And I have no intention of handing off my responsibility to my children to anyone. Not to you. Not now. Not when we're married. Not forty years from now when they all have kids of their own." He paused to consider. "Well, maybe then.

There has to be some limit to the statutes of parenthood.''

Her knees felt as if they were melting as she looked up at his dear smile. ''We're getting...*married?*'' she asked in a breathy voice.

He smiled then, slowly, dearly, and her heart softened with a buttery hope. ''Someday. When you're ready. When I've managed to convince you that I'm crazy in love with you and plan to stay that way the rest of my life.'' His hand came up to cup her chin, his eyes promised her joys she hadn't even known she wanted. ''When you're finally comfortable with the thought that sharing responsibility is a positive experience, especially when it means sharing a life—and a bed—as well.''

She wasn't sure yet, but her instincts told her he had an excellent point. ''I never learned how to share,'' she said, relaxing her face against his wonderful, warm palm. ''At least, that's what Ainsley's been telling me.''

''It's not too late.'' He bent forward and kissed her lightly but thoroughly. ''That's the beauty of it, Miranda. It's not too late. We have all the time we need, but not a moment to waste.'' He kissed her long and passionately, and she began to realize that love came with its own responsibilities, that sharing it was a challenge and a blessing. Sometimes it needed lots of attention and sometimes not as much.

Sometimes laughter, sometimes tears. She had done that once. Alone. Now what she wanted more than anything was to do it again…with Nate. They would write the happy ending to her story together.

"I love you," she said when the kiss ended.

He gathered her close against him, nuzzled her hair. "You know the best thing about this?"

"You're going to get a lot of new shirts?"

"That," he agreed. "And knowing that one day, a few years from now, the children will be grown up and living their own lives, and I'll have you all to myself. I won't have to share you."

She pulled back, but not too far. She was never going that far again. "What if we decide we want more children?"

"Then, I suppose, the sharing will continue a little longer. But I warn you, twins run in our family."

"Really?" she teased. "Mine, too."

"Does that make us a perfect match?"

"You'll have to ask Ainsley about that, but I'm pretty sure she'll say yes."

"And you, Miranda? What do you say?"

She drew back, smiled up at him. "I say…you should take off that shirt."

He reached for the buttons. "I knew you couldn't keep your hands off this shirt. It's a pretty bad stain, isn't it?"

"Yes," she agreed, reaching up to help him. "I'm

afraid it's going to have to soak for a long time. You may not get back to the coffeehouse for hours. Do you think Nick will be able to manage without you?''

Nate began stripping off the shirt, his smile edging up to a grin. ''A dose of the real world will be good for him. Besides, he has the kids there to help.'' He handed her the shirt...which she promptly tossed across the pool table.

Her hands slid across Nate's muscled chest, delighted in his soft intake of breath, thrilled when his hands came up to capture hers and hold them close. ''Don't you think that's a little too much responsibility for him? He's still a child, himself.''

''It's about time he grew up.'' Nate whispered a kiss along the curve of her ear. ''And about time you got some club soda on that shirt, don't you think? I know you're thinking about it.''

He was right. Try as she might, the stain was on her mind. But a woman could change her mind. Miranda knew she had options and the one in front of her was so much more important. Not to mention enticing. ''Don't worry,'' she told him. ''I have a plan.''

''I can't wait to hear it.''

She smiled, slid her hands up and around his neck, pulled his lips down to hers. ''Let me show you,'' she whispered.

Then she kissed him, and Nate, demonstrating a remarkable knack for knowing when to start sharing the responsibility, kissed her back.

As plans went, Miranda had to deem this one a complete success.

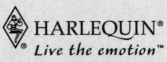

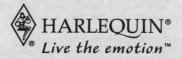

If you enjoyed what you just read,
then we've got an offer you can't resist!

Take 2 bestselling
love stories FREE!
Plus get a FREE surprise gift!

Clip this page and mail it to Harlequin Reader Service®

IN U.S.A.
3010 Walden Ave.
P.O. Box 1867
Buffalo, N.Y. 14240-1867

IN CANADA
P.O. Box 609
Fort Erie, Ontario
L2A 5X3

YES! Please send me 2 free Harlequin American Romance® novels and my free surprise gift. After receiving them, if I don't wish to receive anymore, I can return the shipping statement marked cancel. If I don't cancel, I will receive 4 brand-new novels every month, before they're available in stores! In the U.S.A., bill me at the bargain price of $3.99 plus 25¢ shipping & handling per book and applicable sales tax, if any*. In Canada, bill me at the bargain price of $4.74 plus 25¢ shipping & handling per book and applicable taxes**. That's the complete price and a savings of at least 10% off the cover prices—what a great deal! I understand that accepting the 2 free books and gift places me under no obligation ever to buy any books. I can always return a shipment and cancel at any time. Even if I never buy another book from Harlequin, the 2 free books and gift are mine to keep forever.

154 HDN DNT7
354 HDN DNT9

Name	(PLEASE PRINT)	
Address	Apt.#	
City	State/Prov.	Zip/Postal Code

* Terms and prices subject to change without notice. Sales tax applicable in N.Y.
** Canadian residents will be charged applicable provincial taxes and GST.
   All orders subject to approval. Offer limited to one per household and not valid to
   current Harlequin American Romance® subscribers.
   ® are registered trademarks of Harlequin Enterprises Limited.

AMER02   ©2001 Harlequin Enterprises Limited

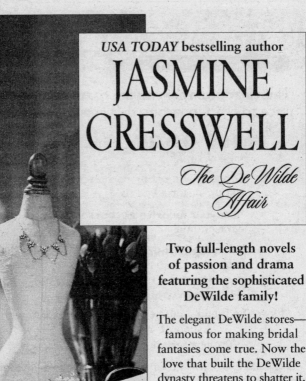

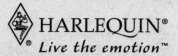

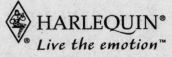